☆☆☆ ARLO & PIPS ☆☆☆

NEW KIDS IN THE FLOCK

ELISE GRAVEL

HARPER alley

An Imprint of HarperCollinsPublishers

HarperAlley is an imprint of HarperCollins Publishers.

Arlo & Pips #3: New Kids in the Flock
Copyright © 2022 by Elise Gravel
All rights reserved. Manufactured in Bosnia and Herzegovina.
No part of this book may be used or reproduced in any manner whatsoever without written permission except
in the case of brief quotations embodied in critical articles and reviews. For information address HarperCollins
Children's Books, a division of HarperCollins Publishers, 195 Broadway, New York, NY 10007.

www.harperalley.com

Library of Congress Control Number 2021948115
ISBN 978-0-06-235125-8 (trade bdg.) — 978-0-06-305079-2 (pbk.)

The artist used Photoshop to create the digital illustrations for this book.

21 22 23 24 25   GPS   10 9 8 7 6 5 4 3 2 1

❖
First Edition

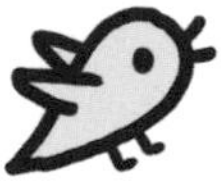

For Enzo,
who is almost an Arlo

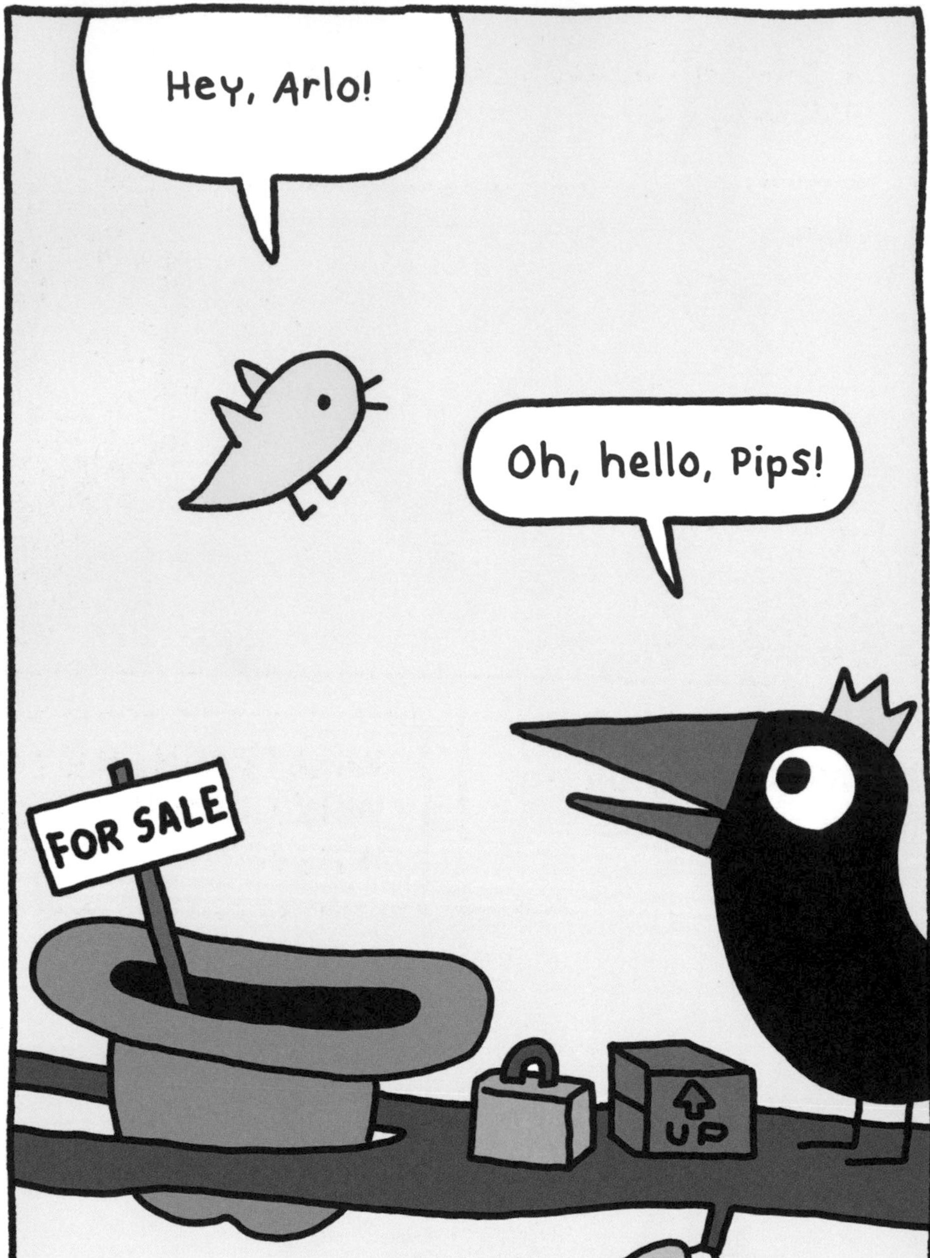
Hey, Arlo!
Oh, hello, Pips!
FOR SALE
UP

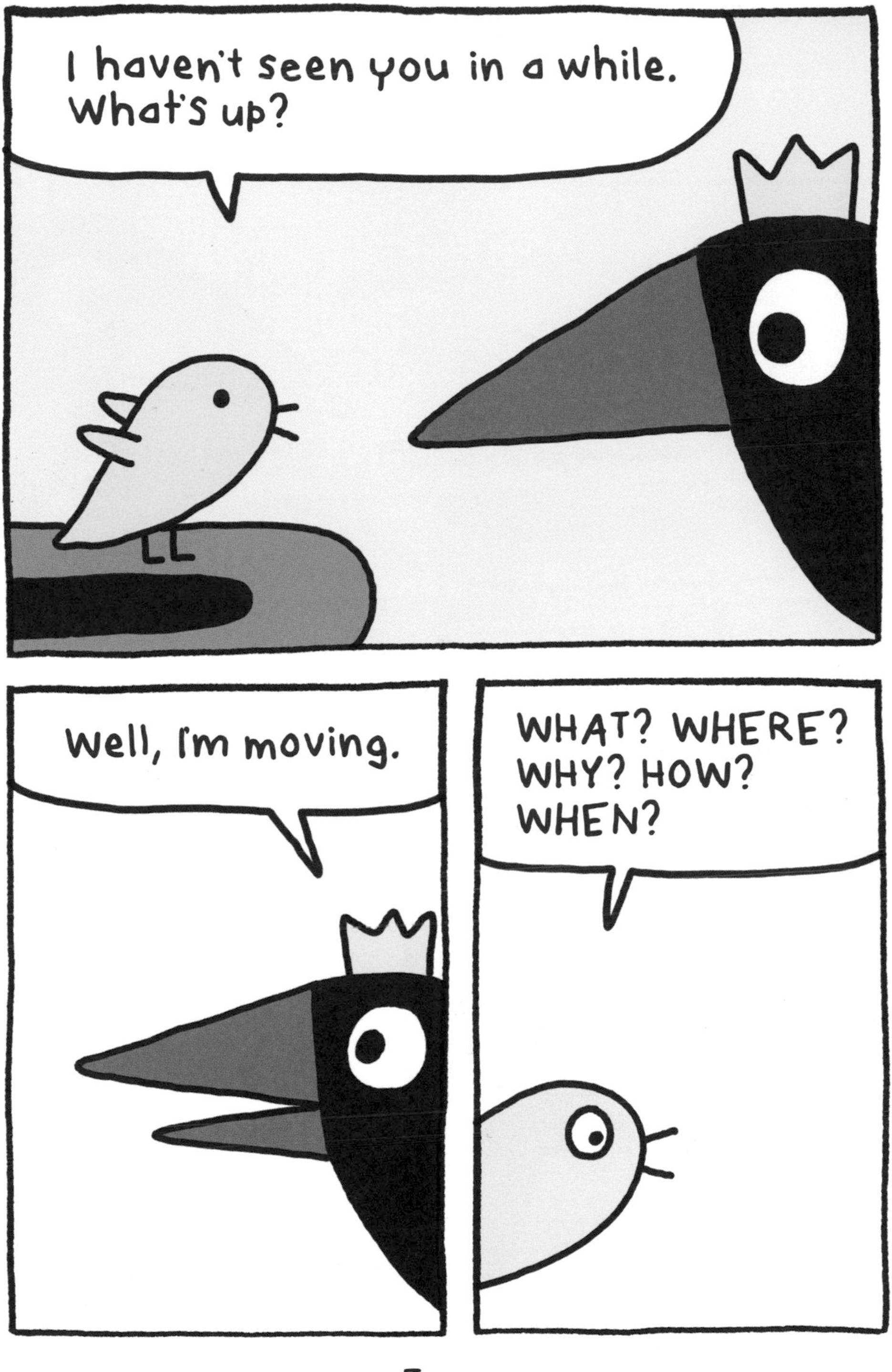
I haven't seen you in a while. What's up?
Well, I'm moving.
WHAT? WHERE? WHY? HOW? WHEN?

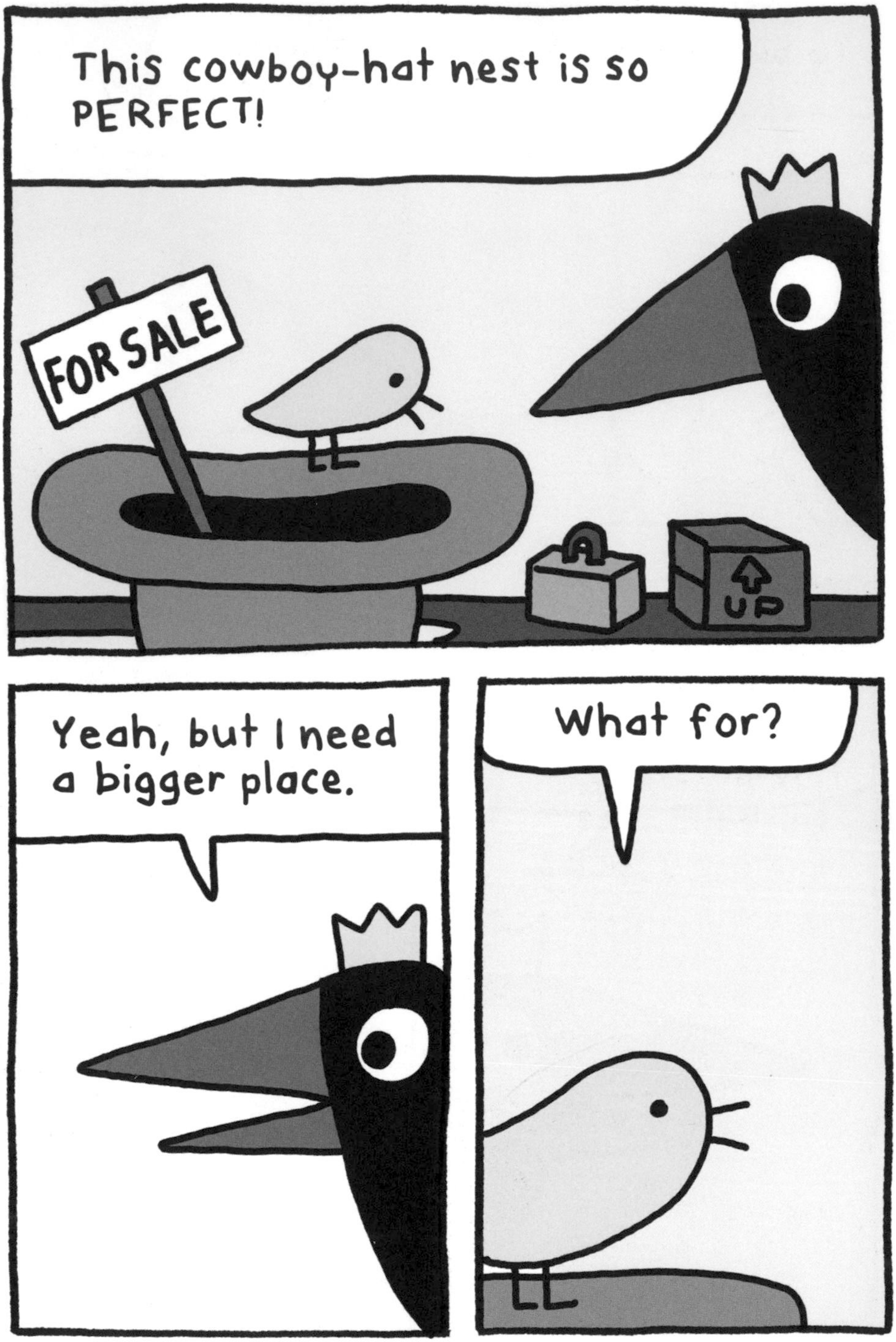
This cowboy-hat nest is so PERFECT!
FOR SALE
UP
Yeah, but I need a bigger place.
What for?

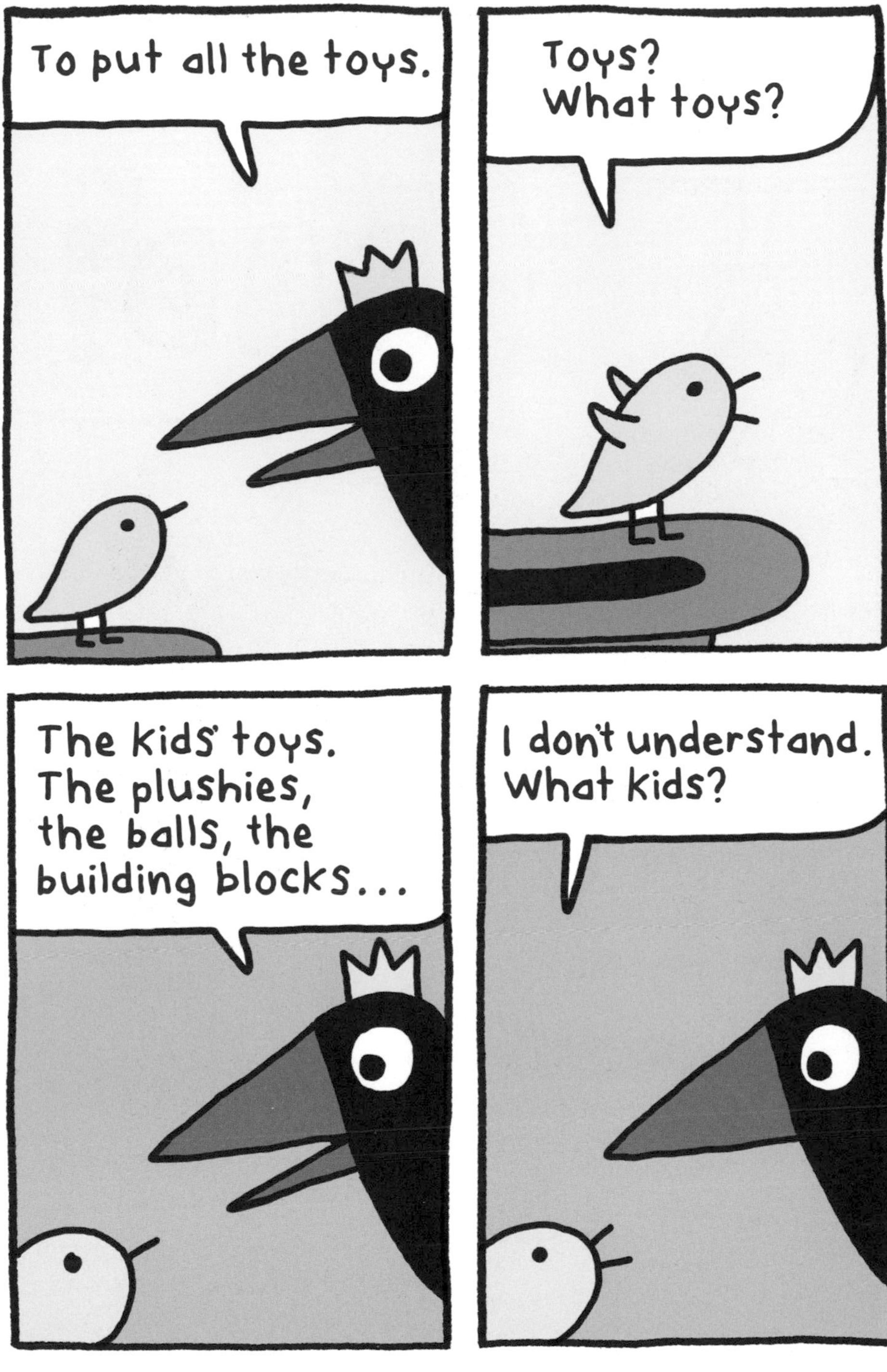
To put all the toys.
Toys? What toys?
The kids' toys. The plushies, the balls, the building blocks...
I don't understand. What kids?

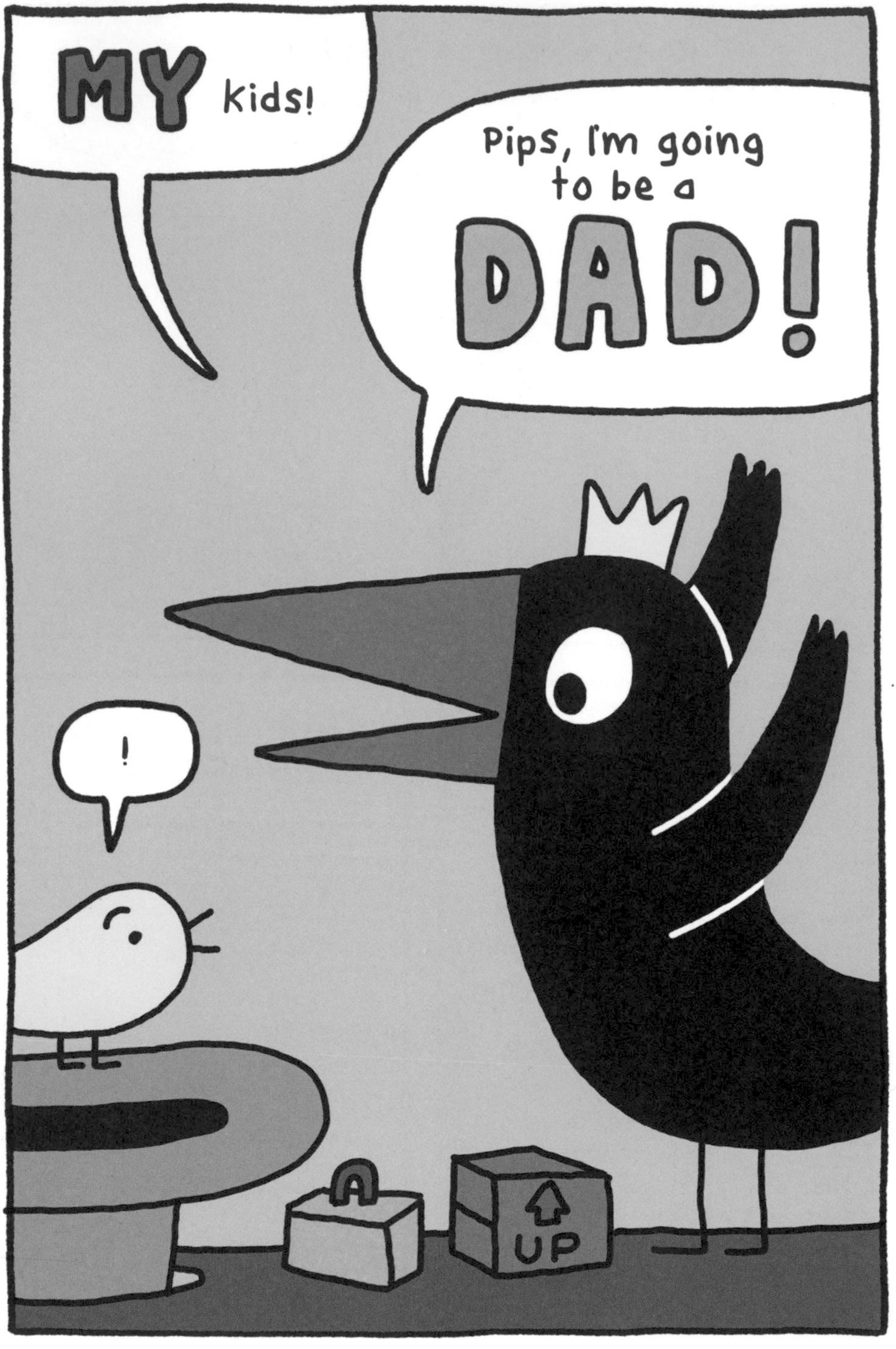
MY kids!
Pips, I'm going to be a DAD!
!
UP

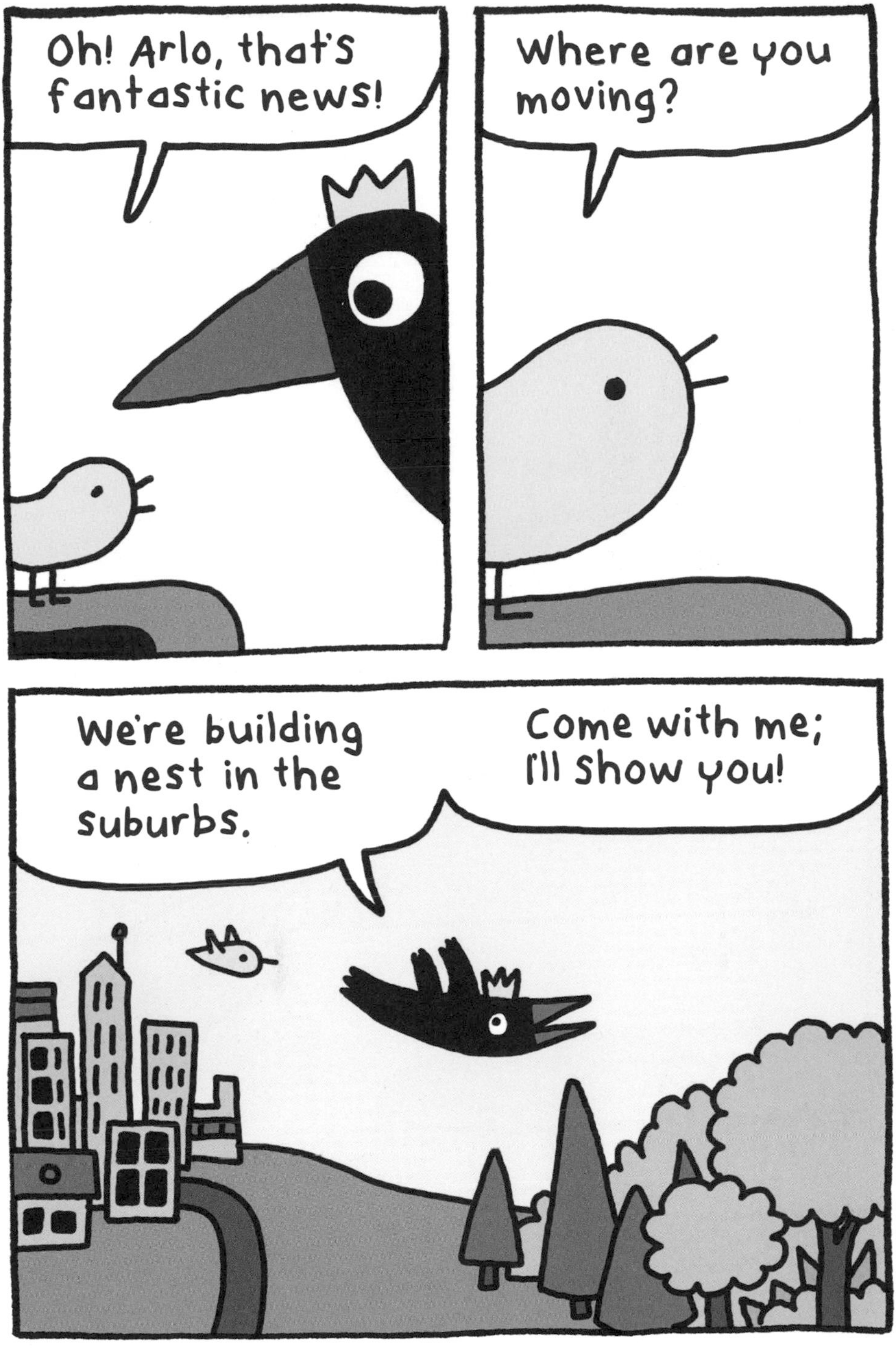

Oh! Arlo, that's fantastic news!
Where are you moving?
We're building a nest in the suburbs.
Come with me; I'll show you!

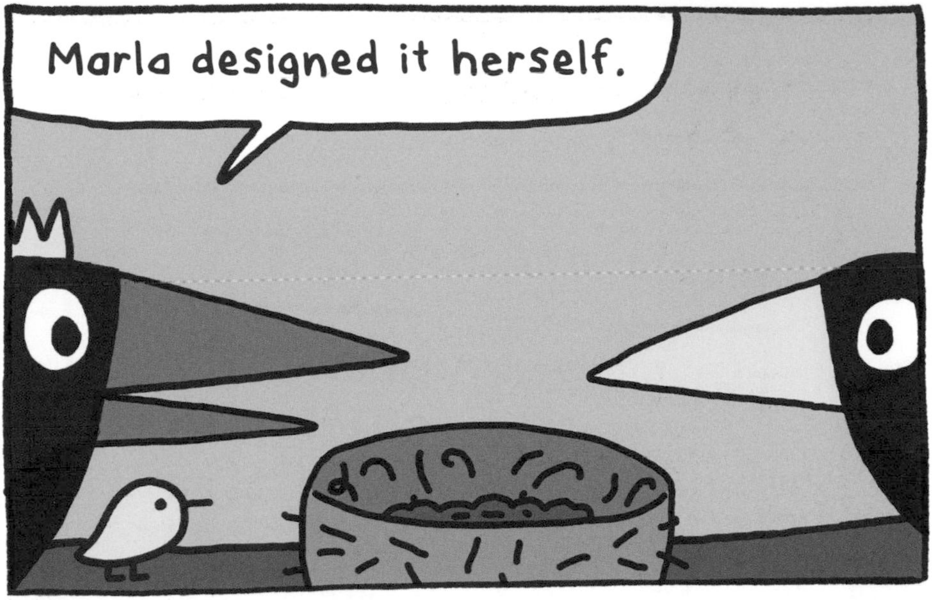
Marla designed it herself.

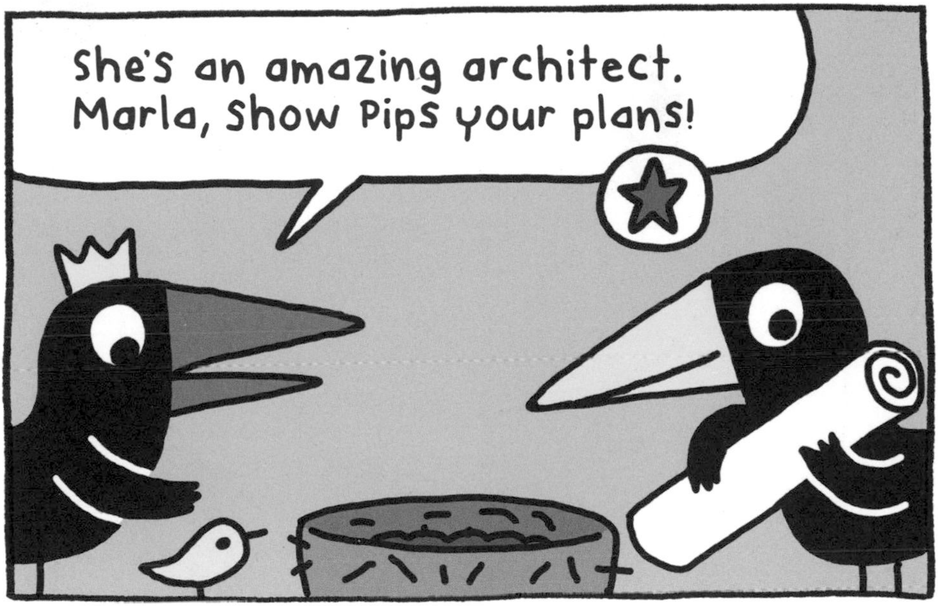
She's an amazing architect. Marla, Show Pips your plans!

★ Crows carefully design their nests and take up to two weeks to build them.

Crows will use whatever soft things they can find to pad their nests.

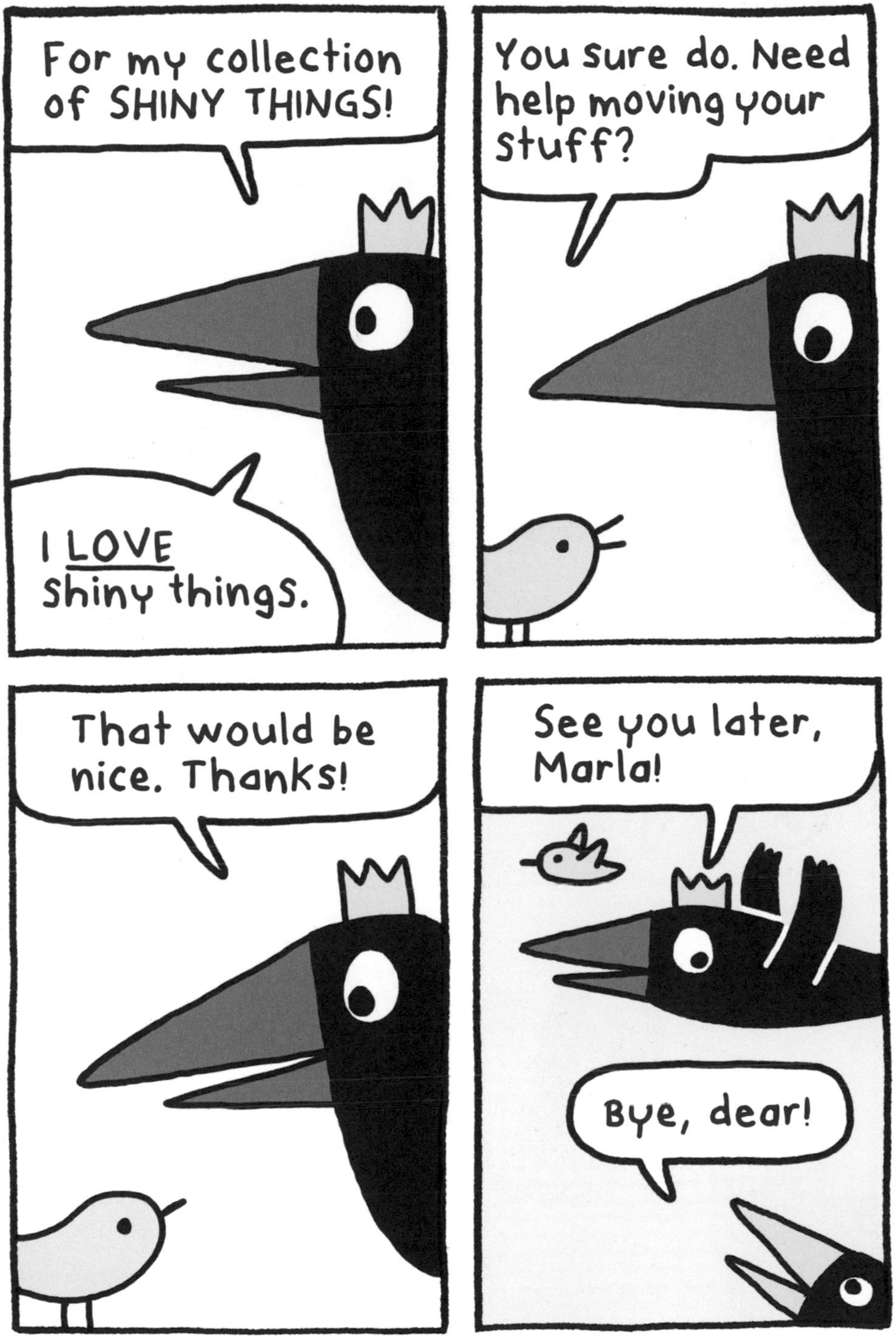
For my collection of SHINY THINGS!
I LOVE shiny things.
You sure do. Need help moving your stuff?
That would be nice. Thanks!
See you later, Marla!
Bye, dear!

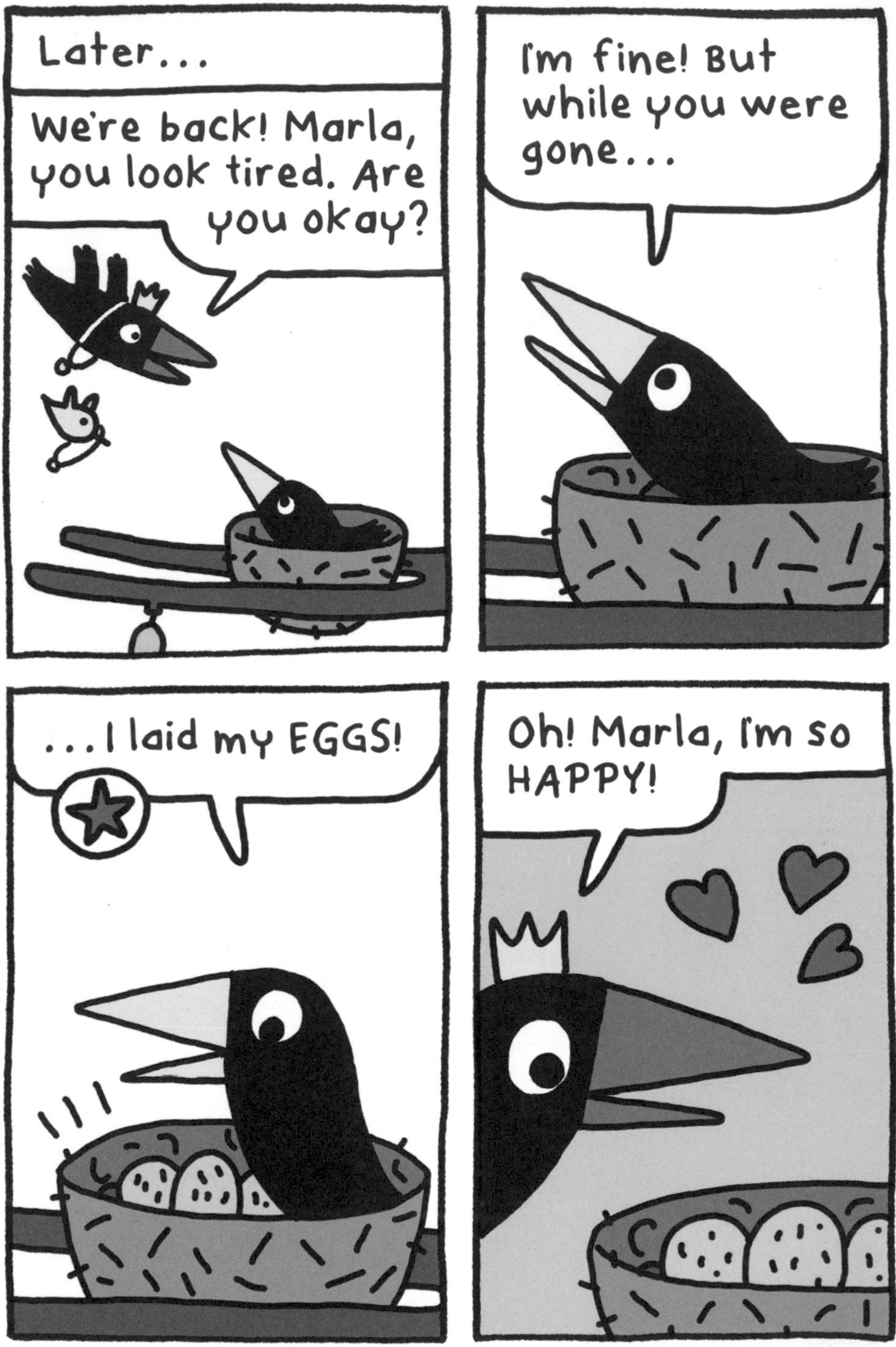
Later...
We're back! Marla, you look tired. Are you okay?
I'm fine! But while you were gone...
...I laid my EGGS!
Oh! Marla, I'm so HAPPY!

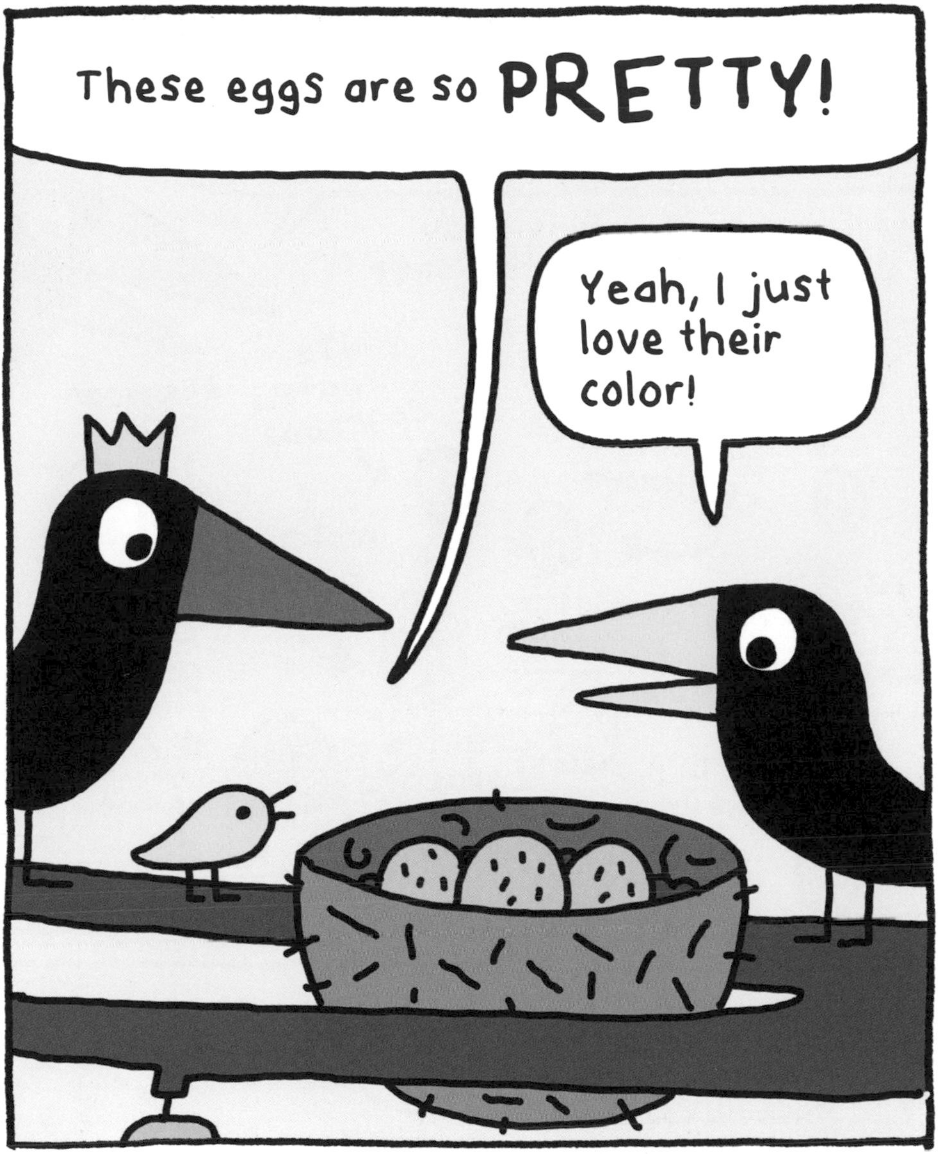
These eggs are so PRETTY!
Yeah, I just love their color!

★ Crows don't lay eggs that fast. They can lay one a day but sometimes take longer, and I need to keep this story going!

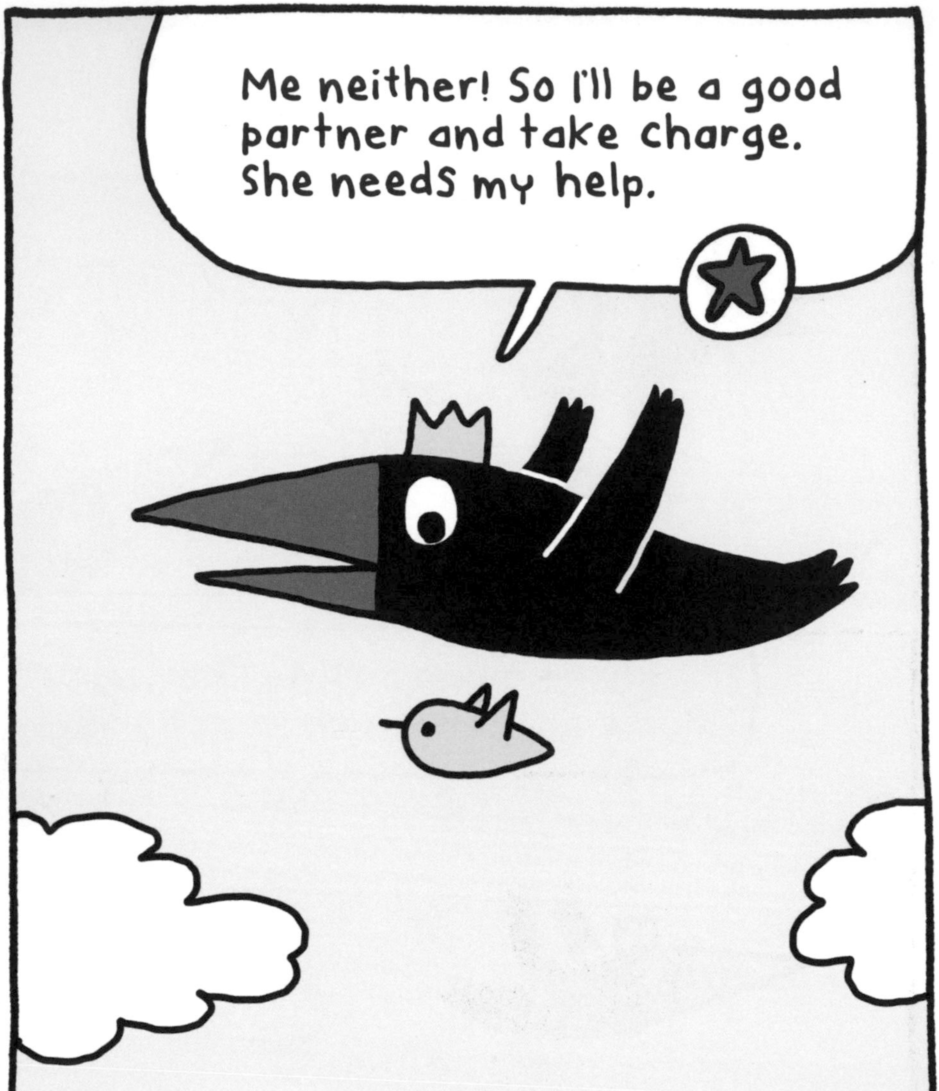
Me neither! So I'll be a good partner and take charge. She needs my help.

Crow dads contribute to the nest and find food for the nesting mom.

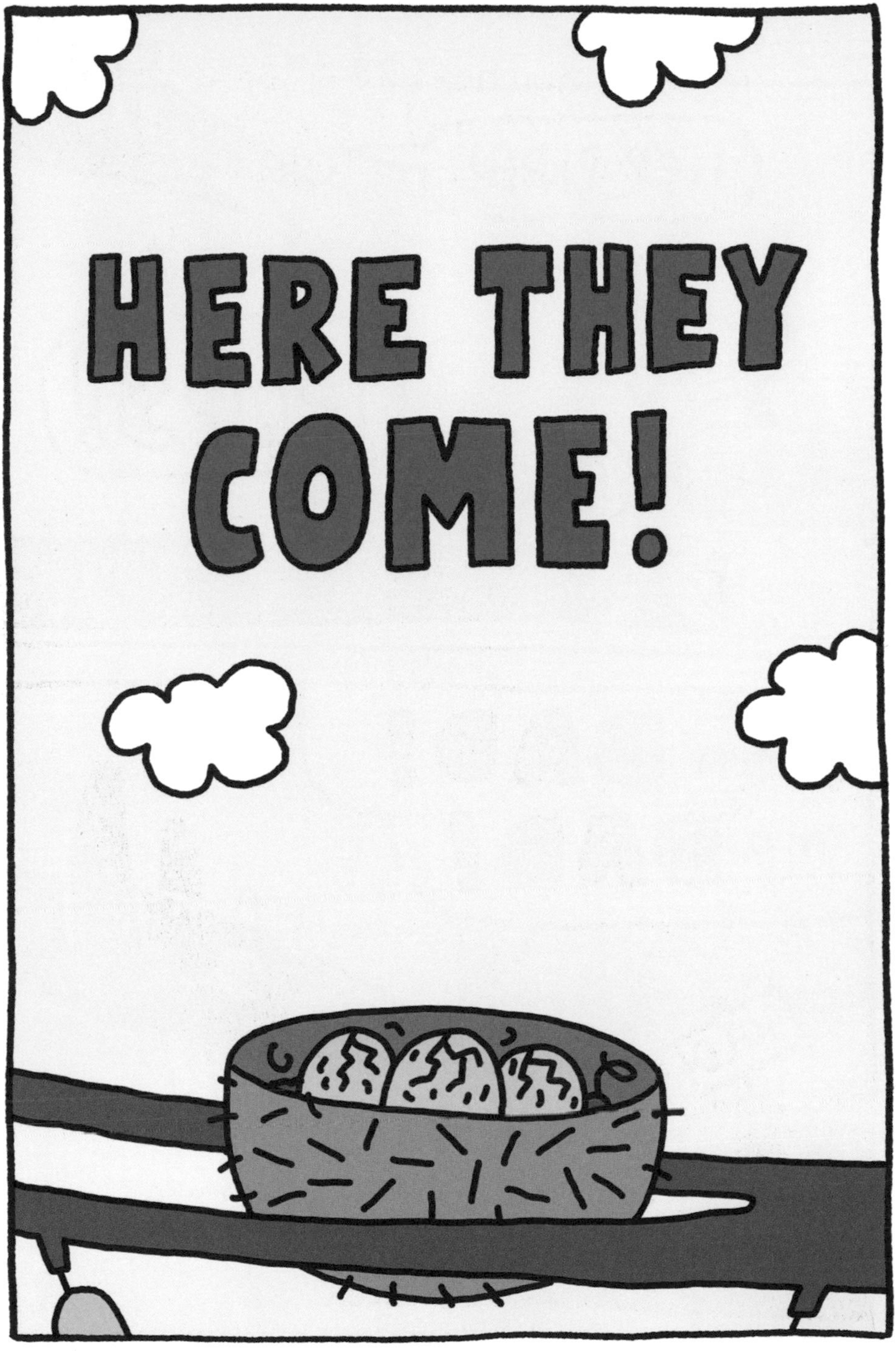
HERE THEY COME!

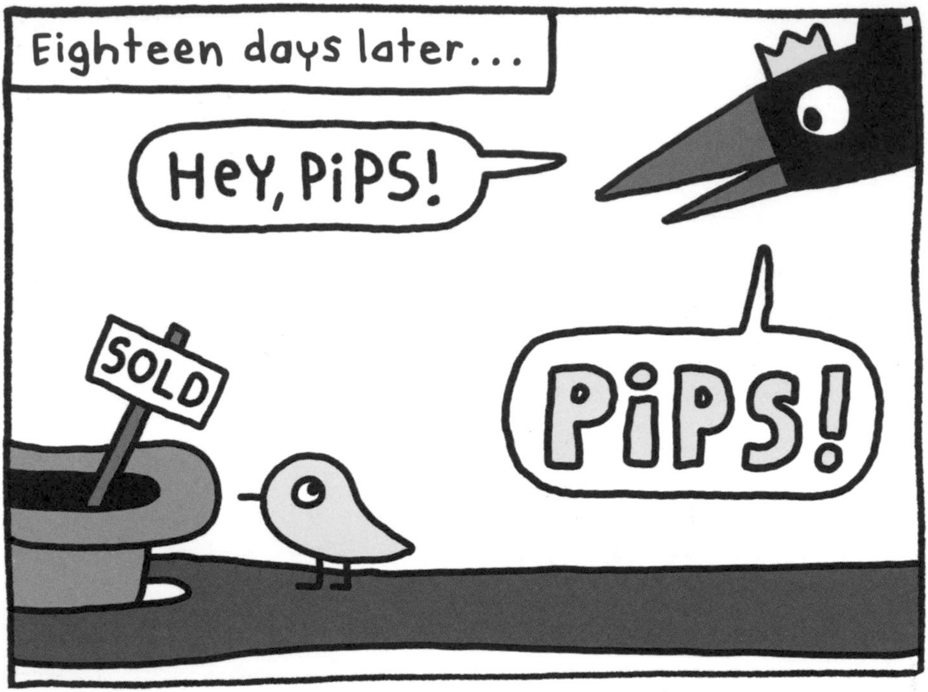
Eighteen days later...
HEY, PiPS!
PiPS!
SOLD

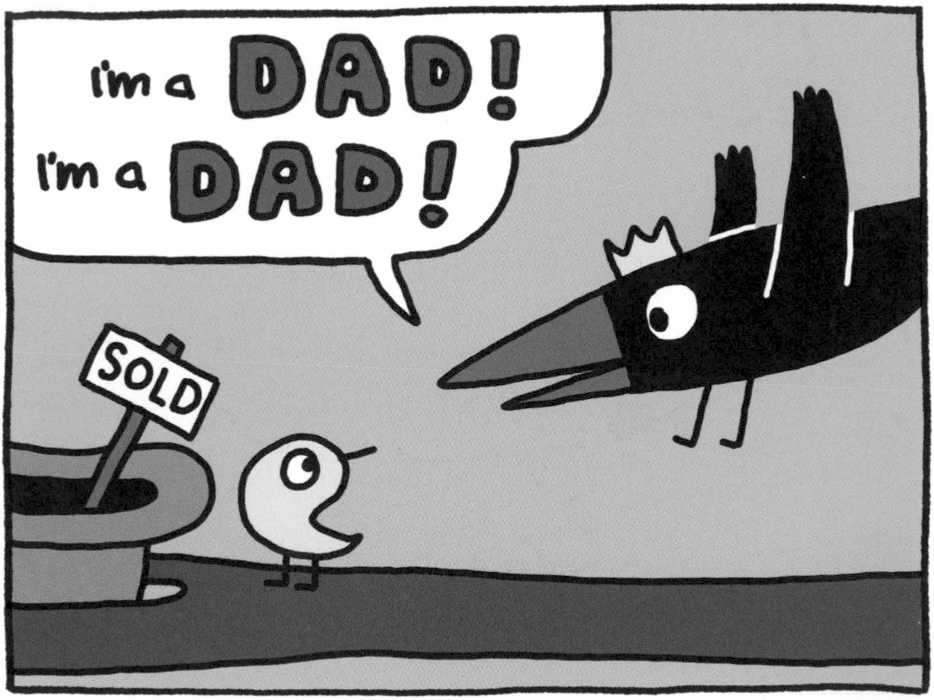
i'm a DAD!
I'm a DAD!
SOLD

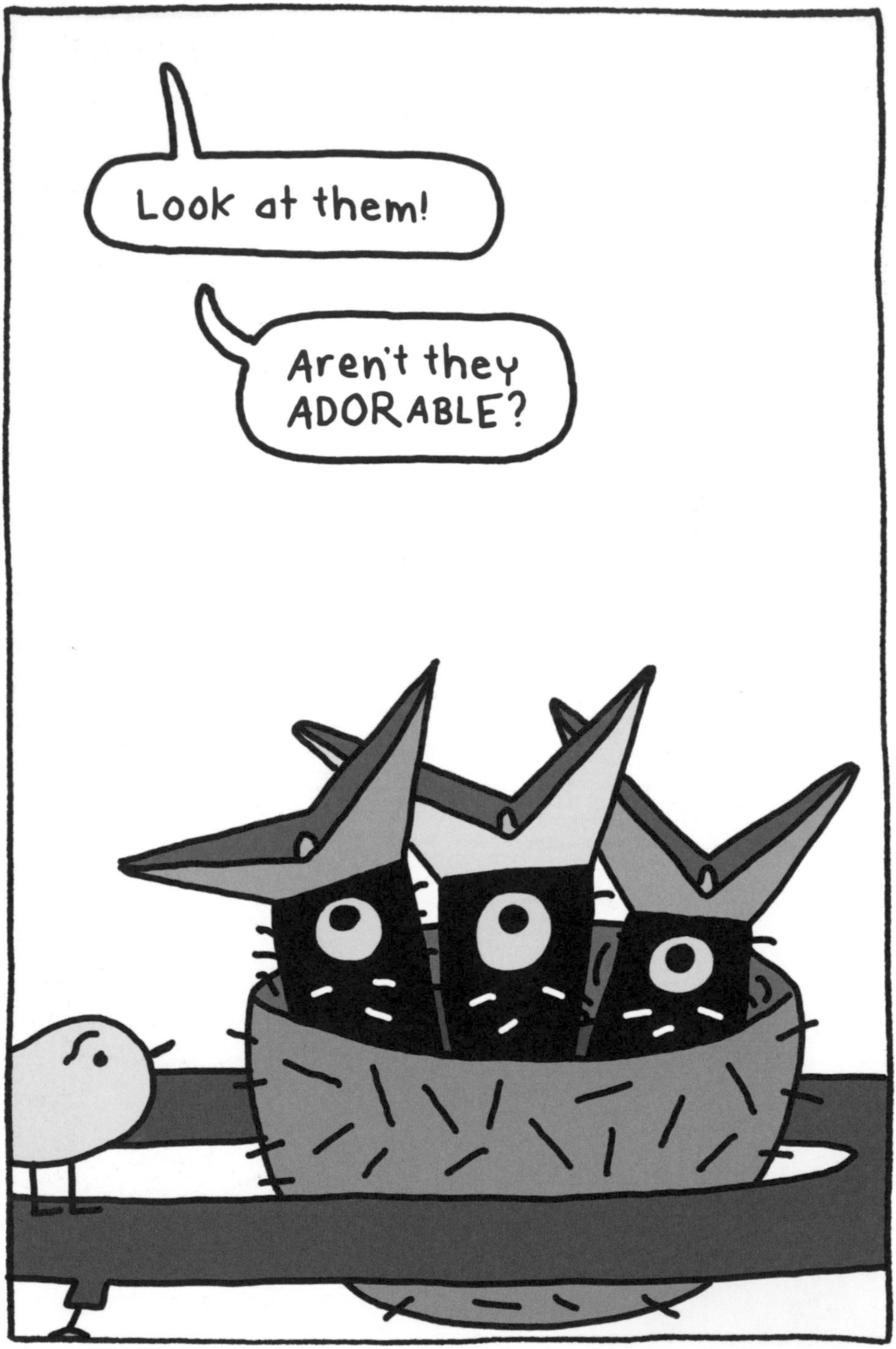
Look at them!
Aren't they ADORABLE?

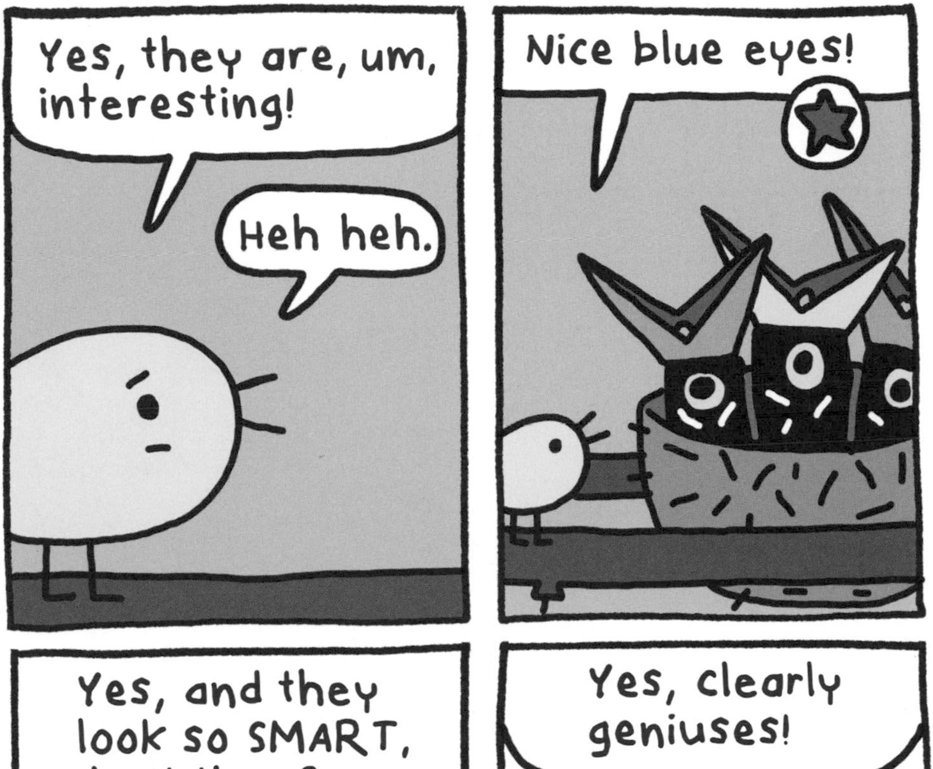
Yes, they are, um, interesting!
Heh heh.
Nice blue eyes!
Yes, and they look so SMART, don't they?
Yes, clearly geniuses!
Do they have names?

★ Newborn crows have blue eyes that turn black as they grow older.

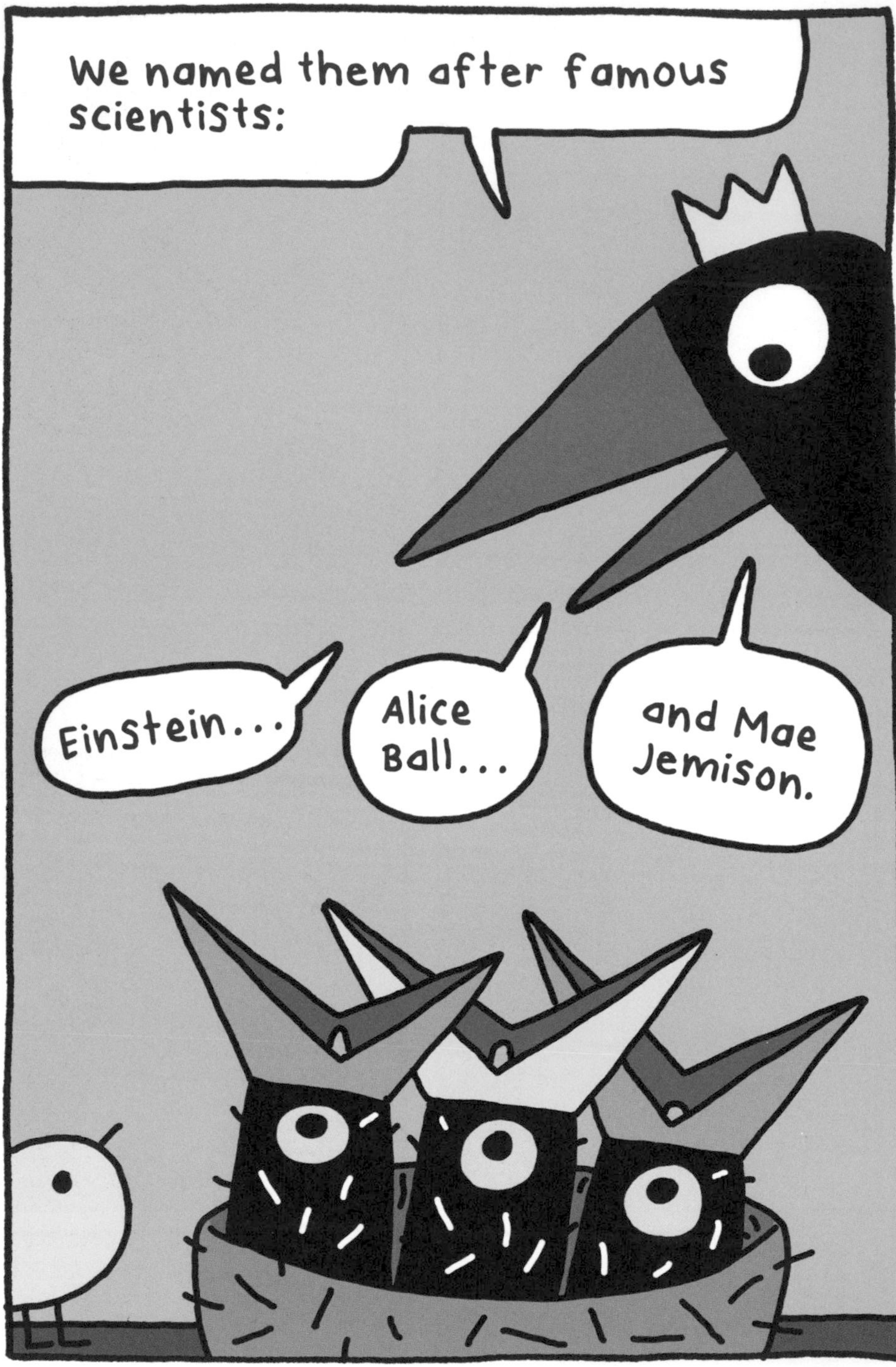
We named them after famous scientists:
Einstein...
Alice Ball...
and Mae Jemison.

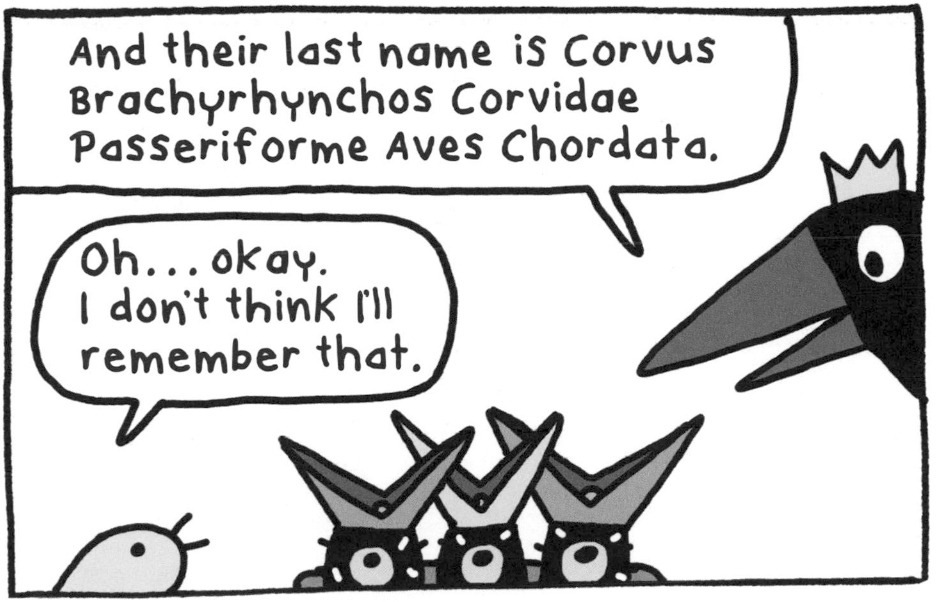
And their last name is Corvus Brachyrhynchos Corvidae Passeriforme Aves Chordata.
Oh... okay. I don't think I'll remember that.

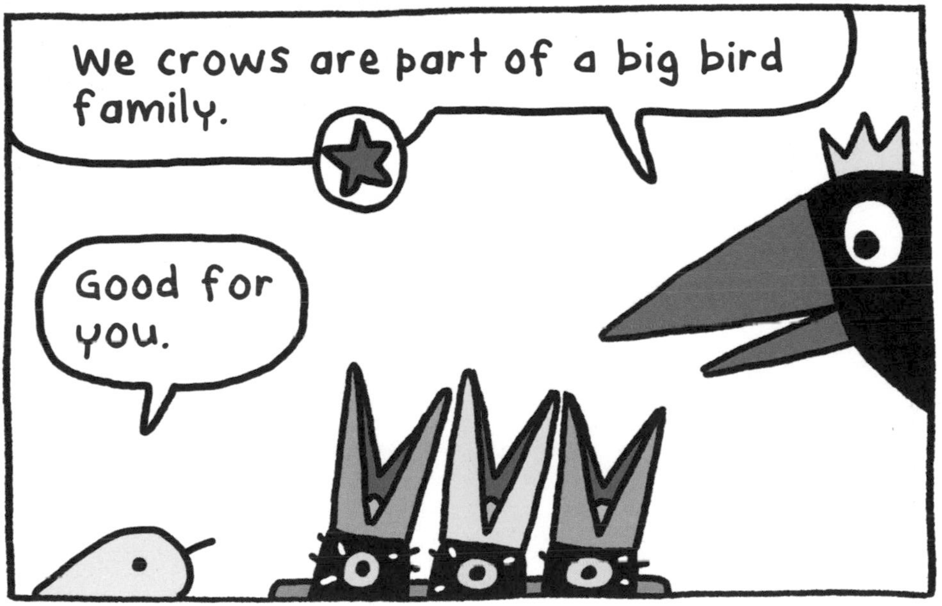
We crows are part of a big bird family.
Good for you.

★ Crows are part of the Corvidae family, which includes ravens, blue jays, magpies, rooks, and nutcrackers.

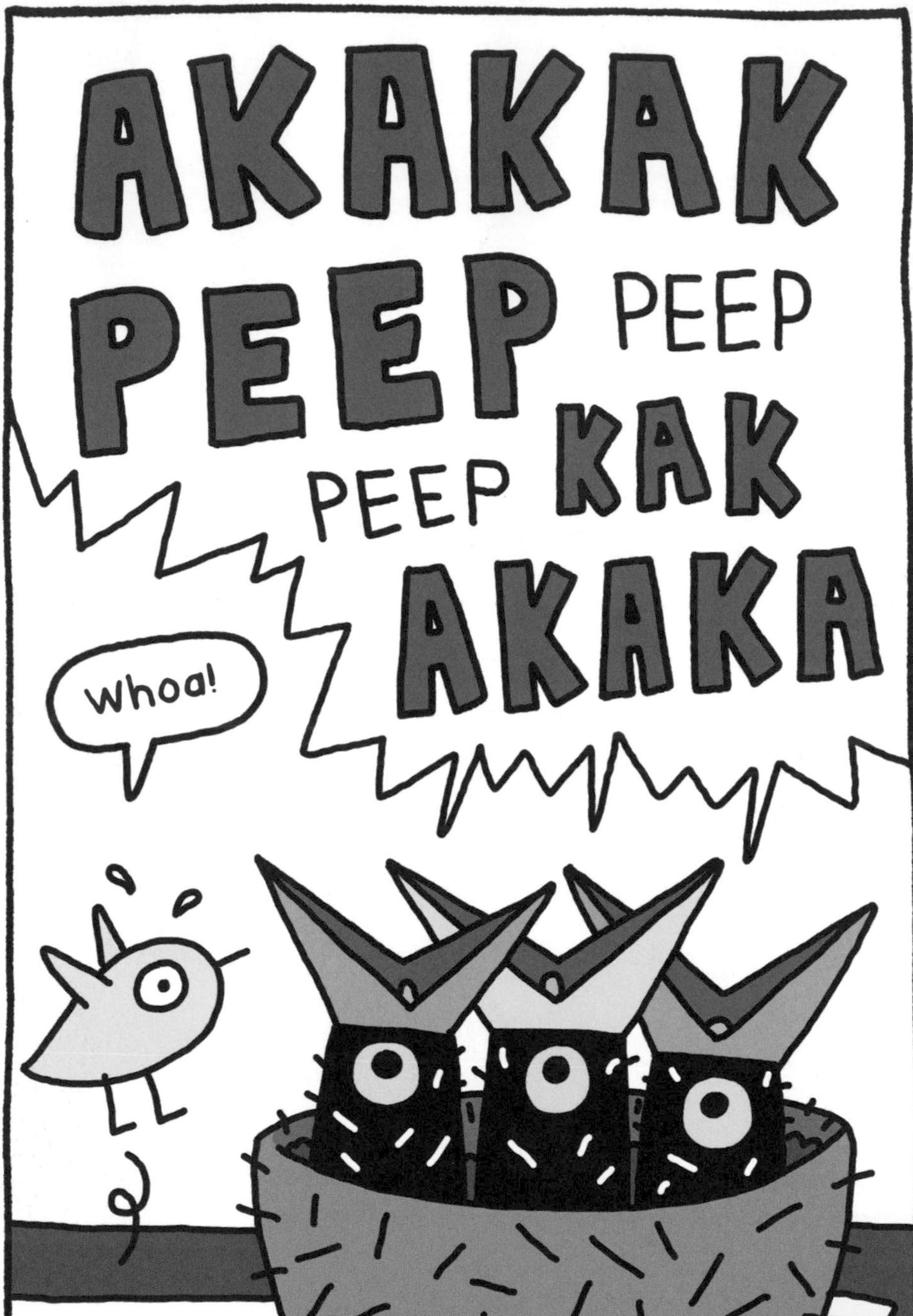
AKAKAK
PEEP PEEP
PEEP KAK
AKAKA
Whoa!

31

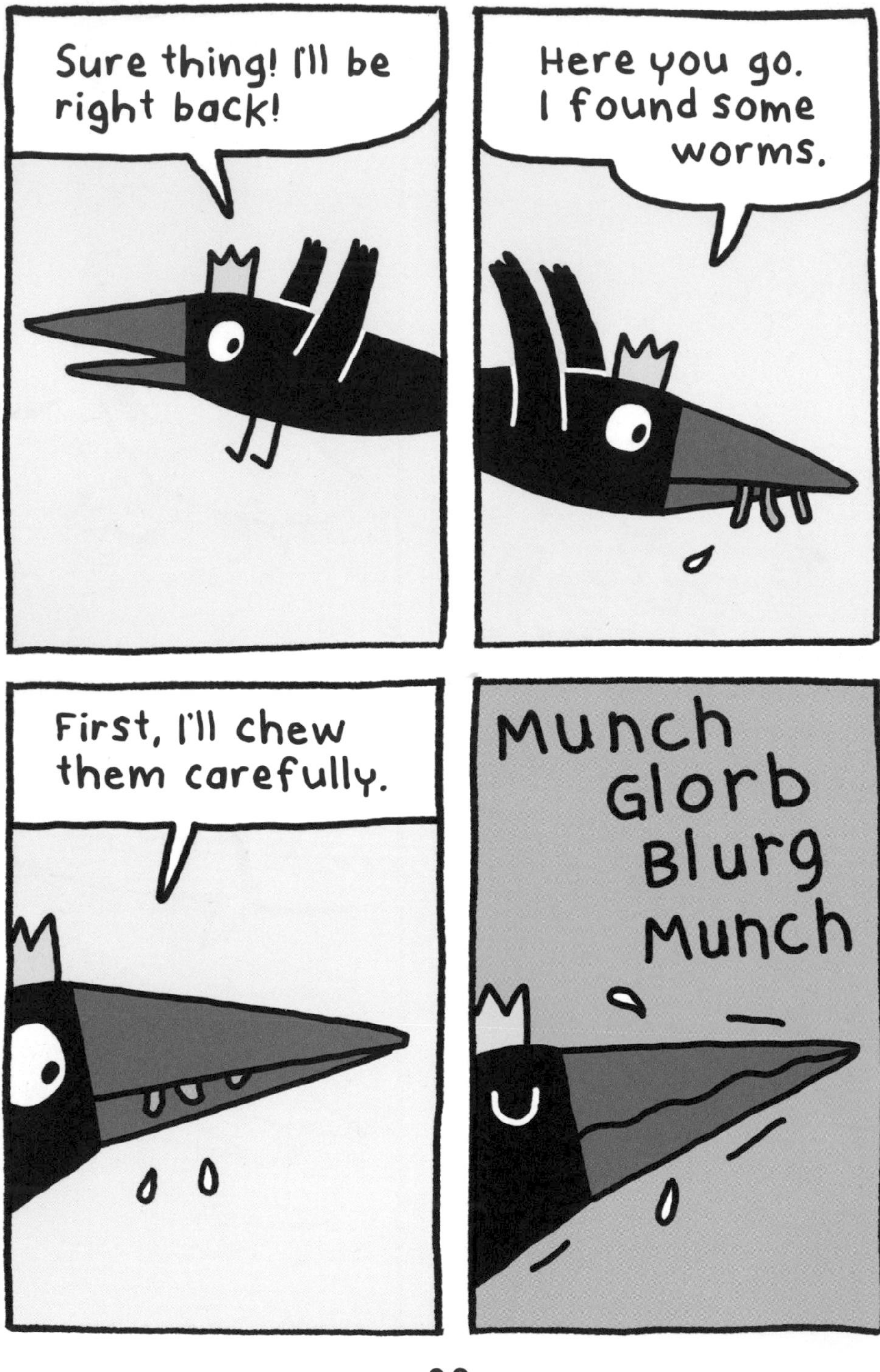
Sure thing! I'll be right back!
Here you go. I found some worms.
First, I'll chew them carefully.
Munch Glorb Blurg Munch

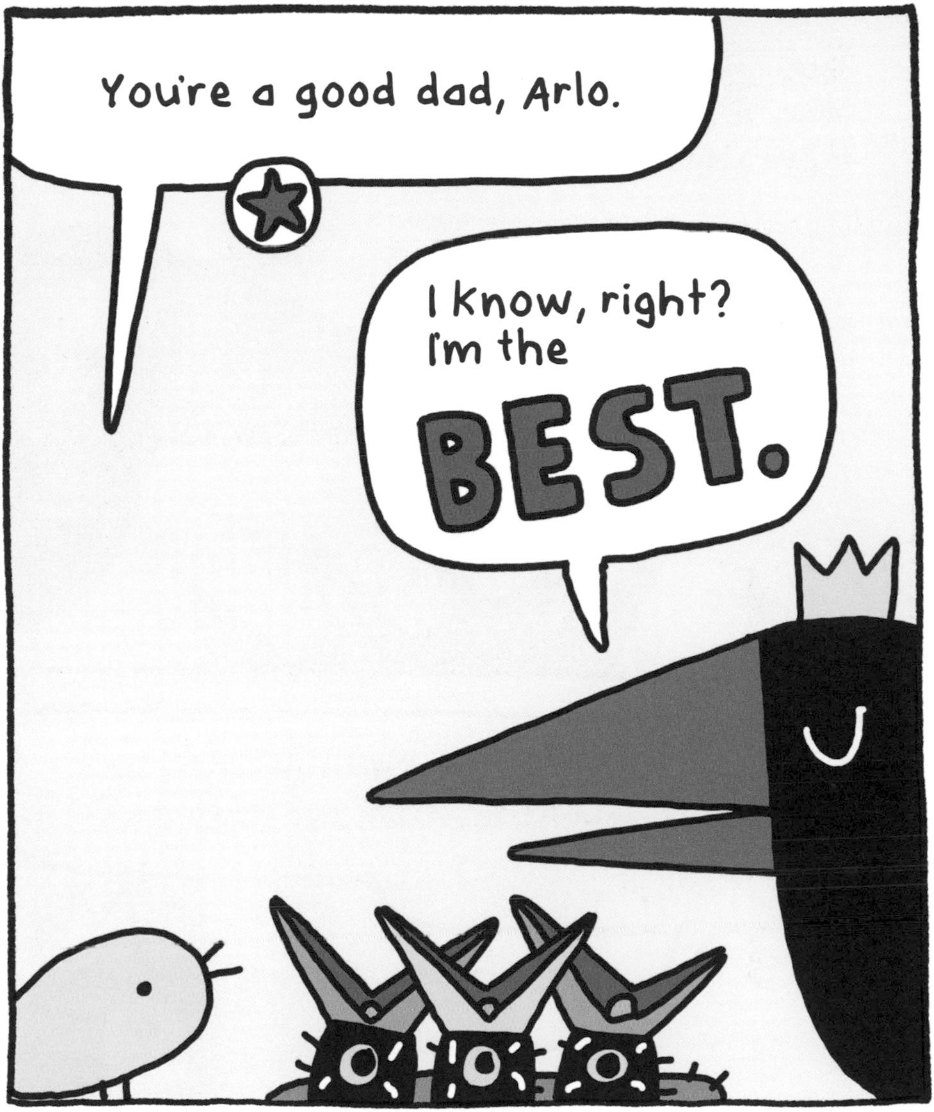
You're a good dad, Arlo.
I know, right? I'm the BEST.

Unlike other bird species, crow dads are good parents. They help feed and educate their babies.

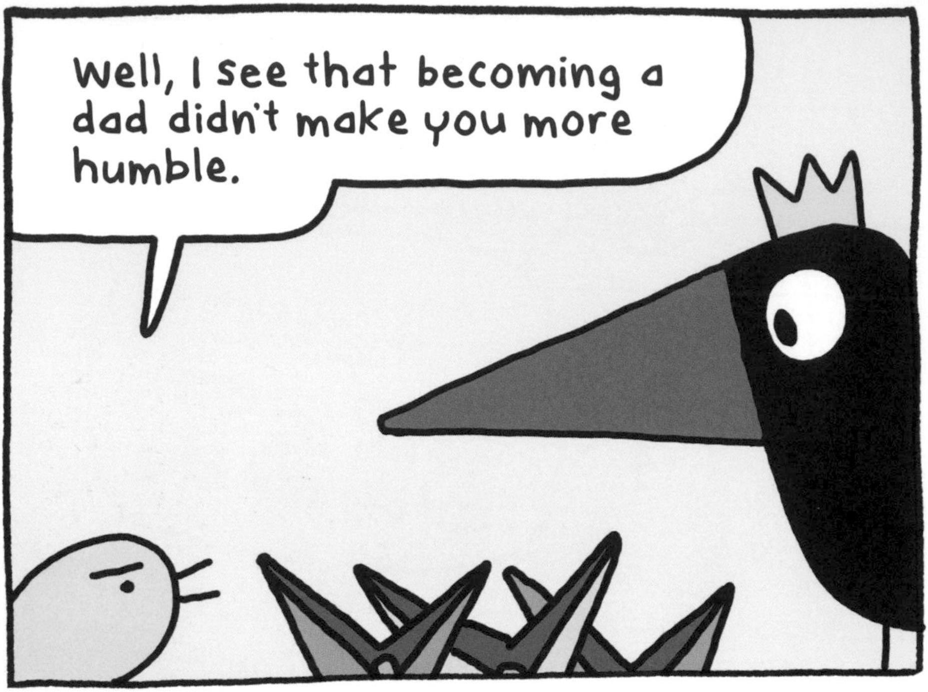
Well, I see that becoming a dad didn't make you more humble.

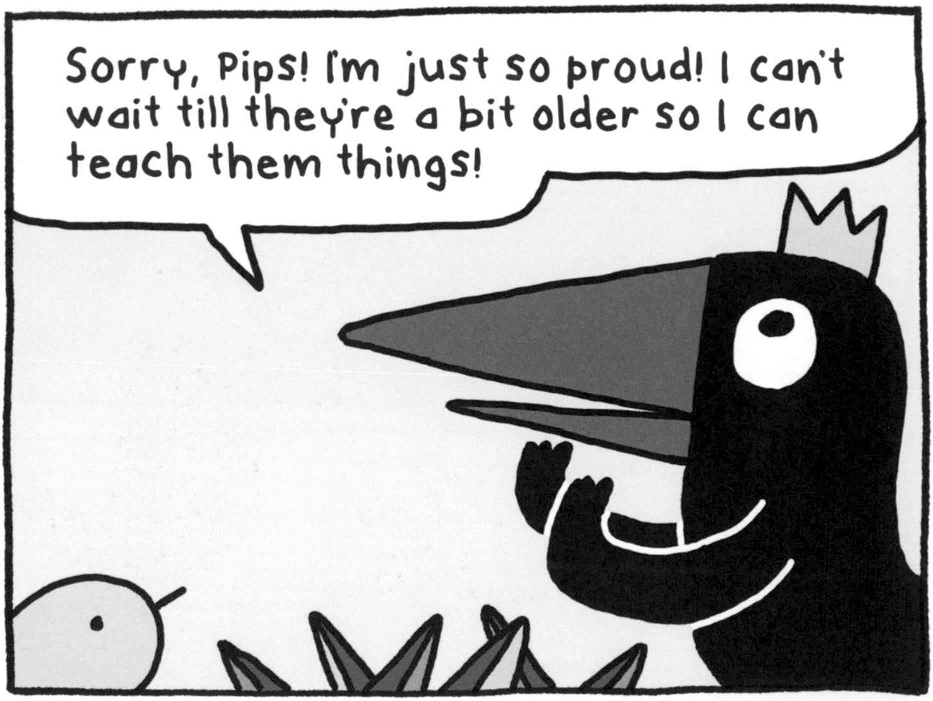
Sorry, Pips! I'm just so proud! I can't wait till they're a bit older so I can teach them things!

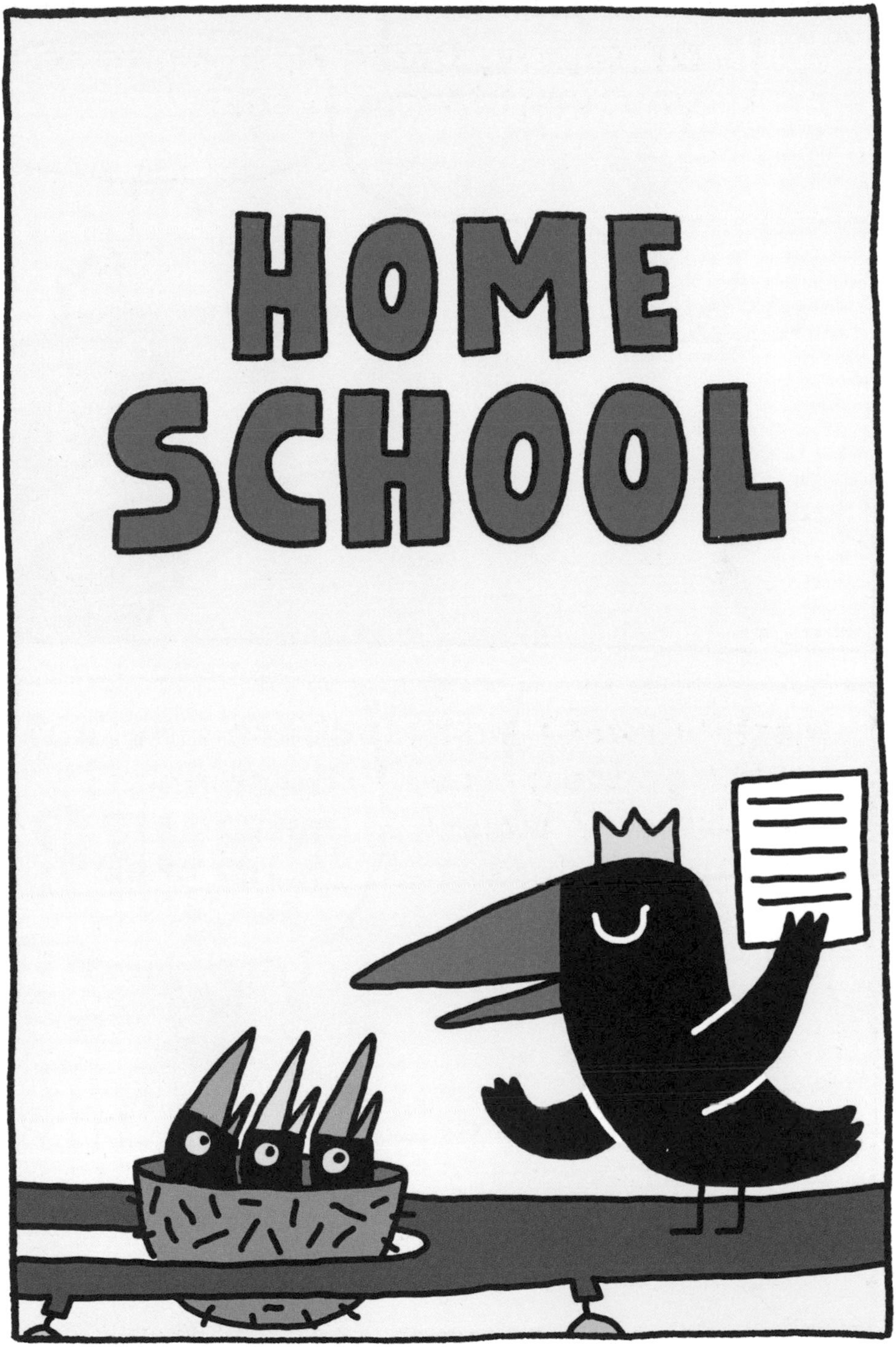
HOME
SCHOOL

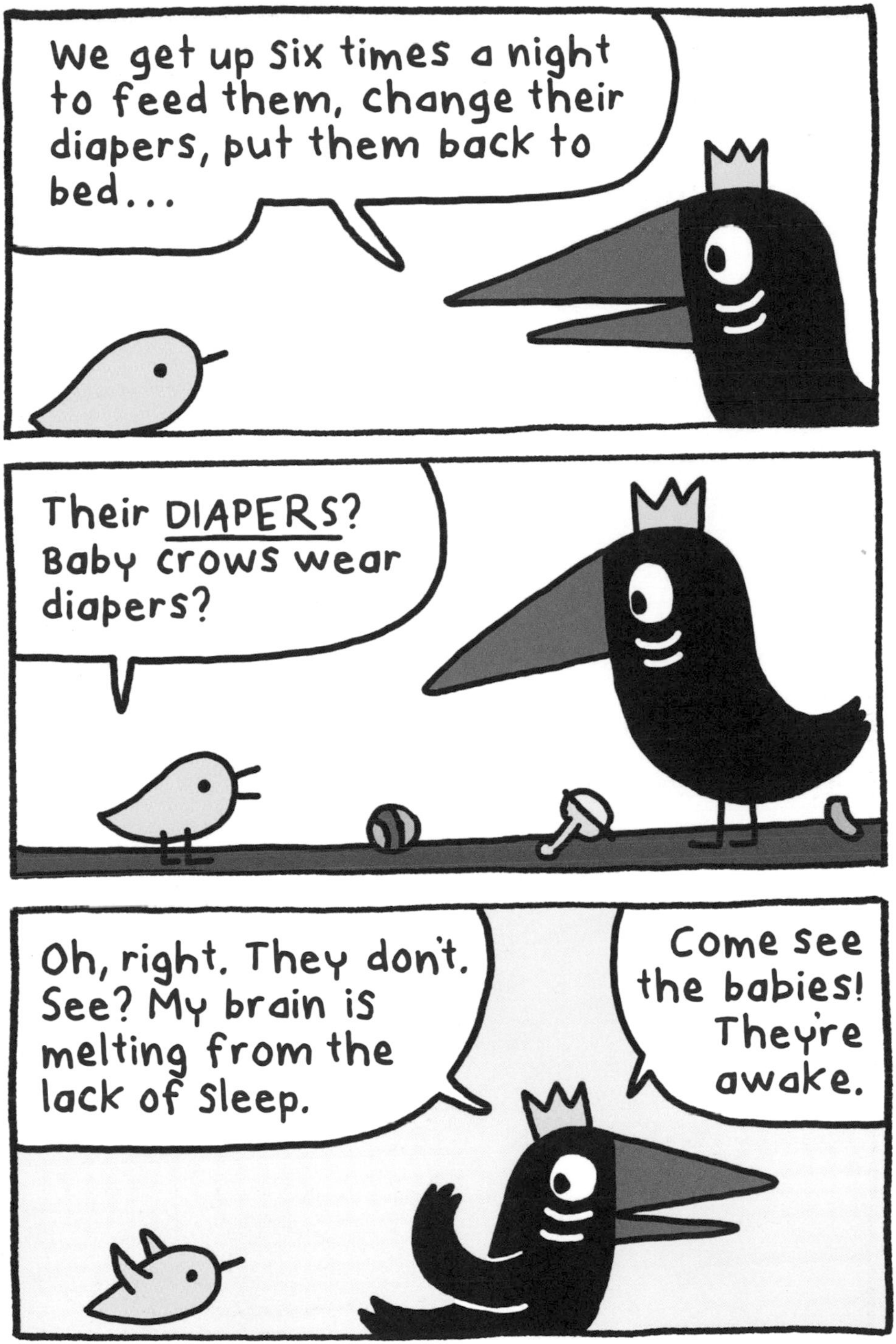
We get up six times a night to feed them, change their diapers, put them back to bed...
Their DIAPERS? Baby crows wear diapers?
Oh, right. They don't. See? My brain is melting from the lack of sleep.
Come see the babies! They're awake.

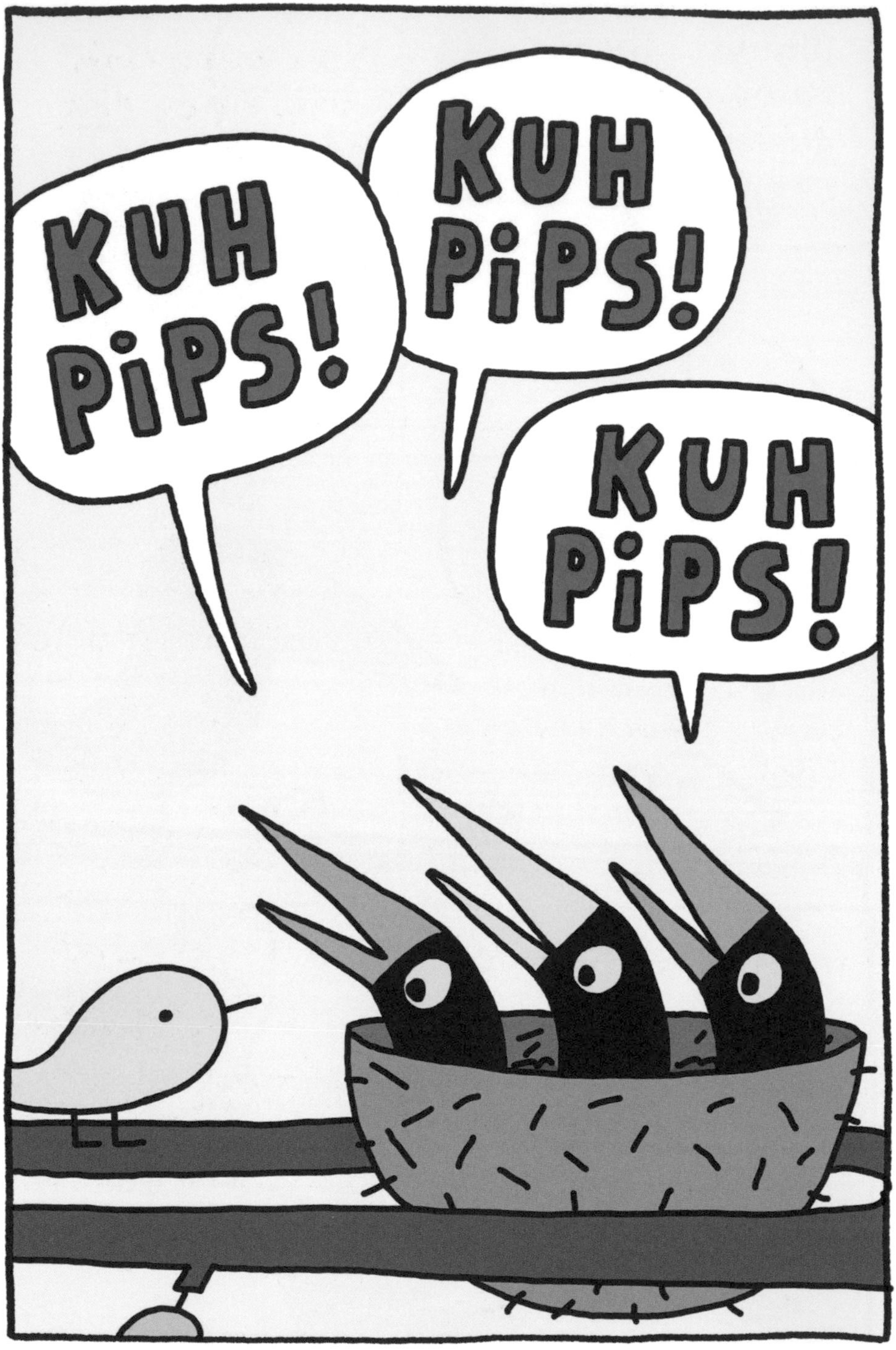
KUH PiPS!
KUH PiPS!
KUH PiPS!

Baby crows actually "talk" to each other. They can learn more than twenty calls.

44

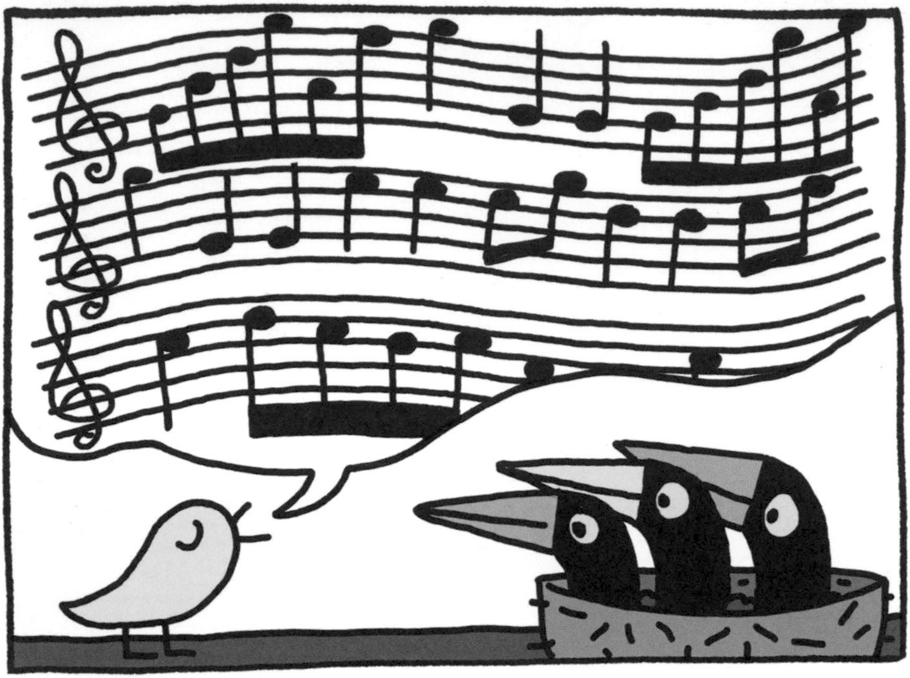

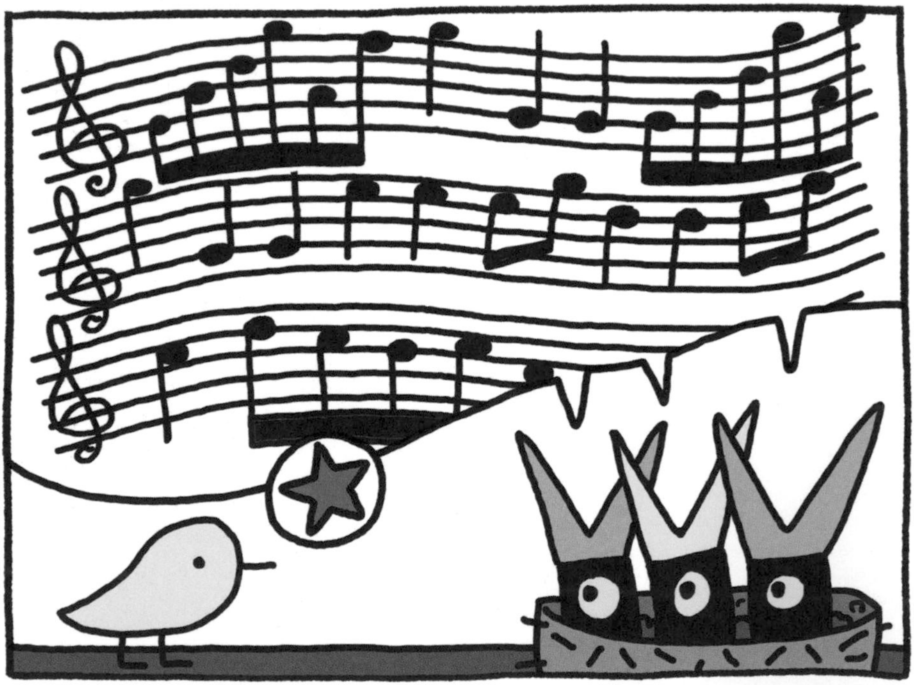

Crows can imitate other birds' songs almost perfectly!

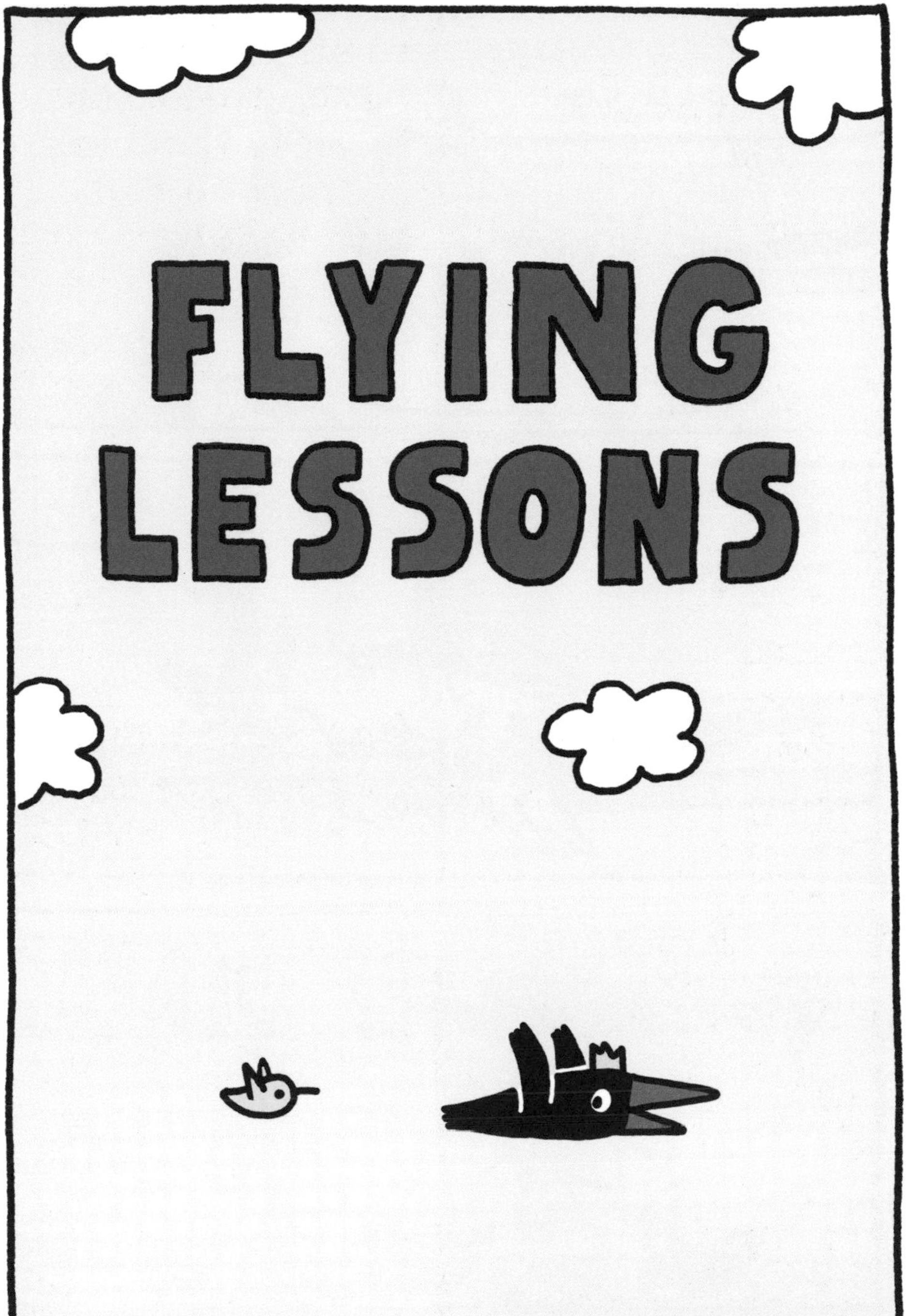
FLYING
LESSONS

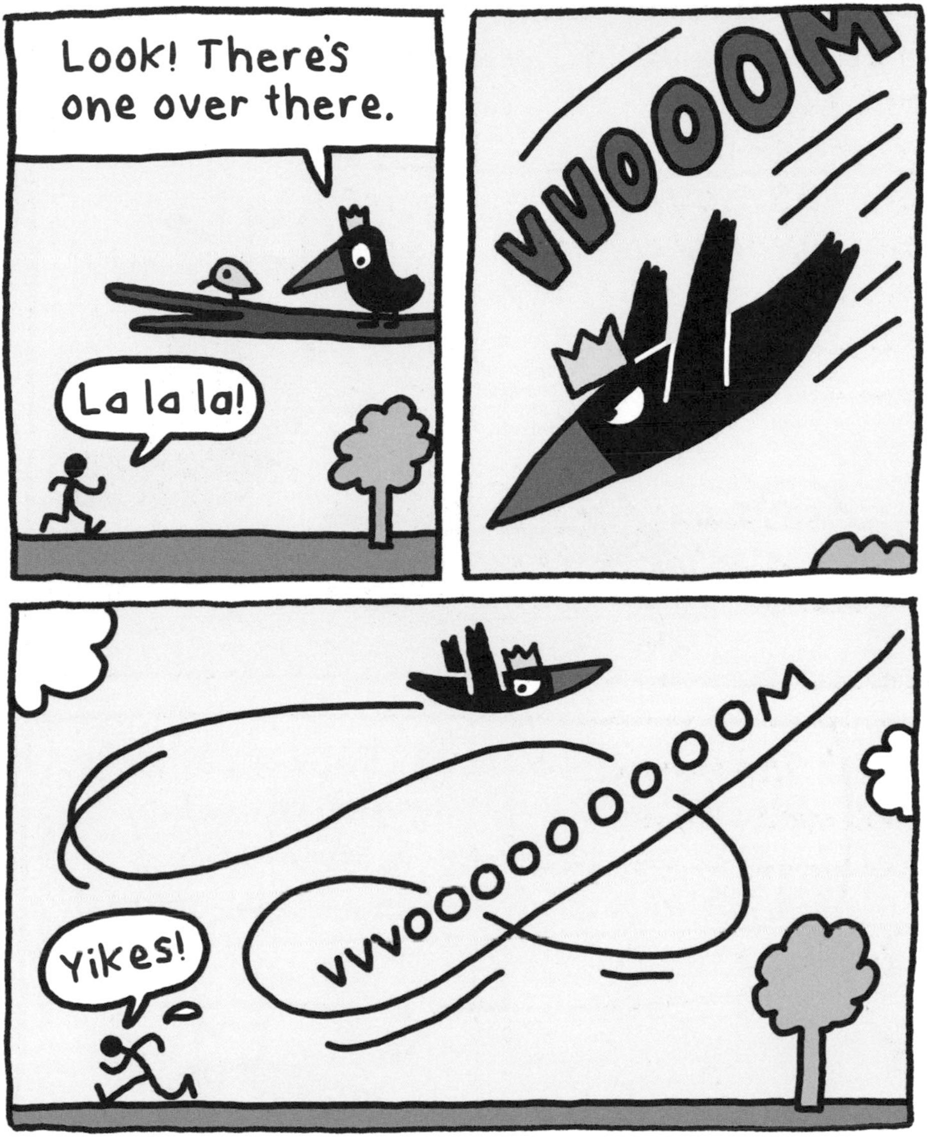

Look! There's one over there.
La la la!
VVOOOM
VVVOOOOOOOOOM
Yikes!

If you see a young crow on the ground, leave them alone. They're probably safe. And if a crow dive-bombs you, move away. They are protecting their babies.

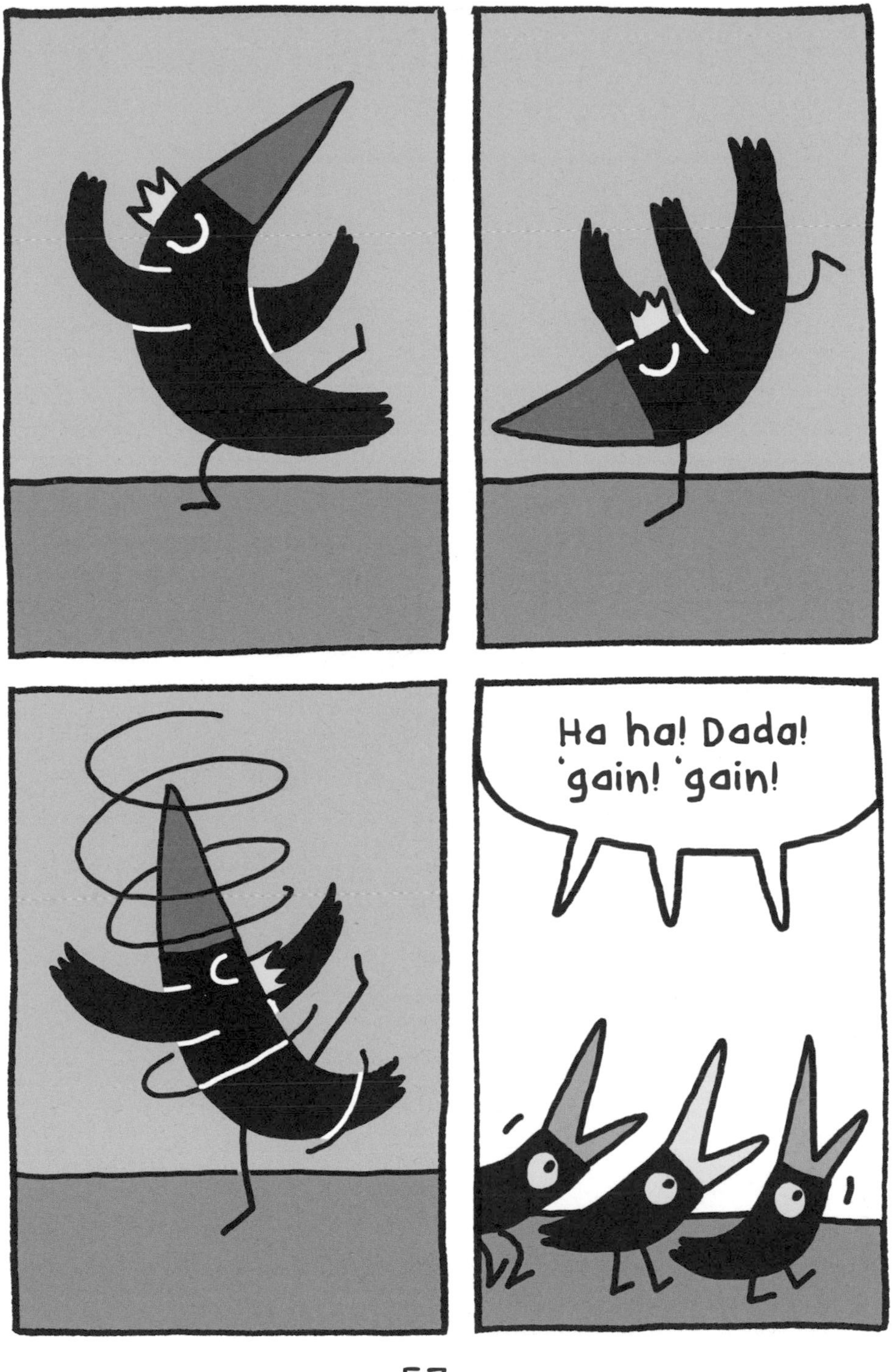
Ha ha! Dada! 'gain! 'gain!

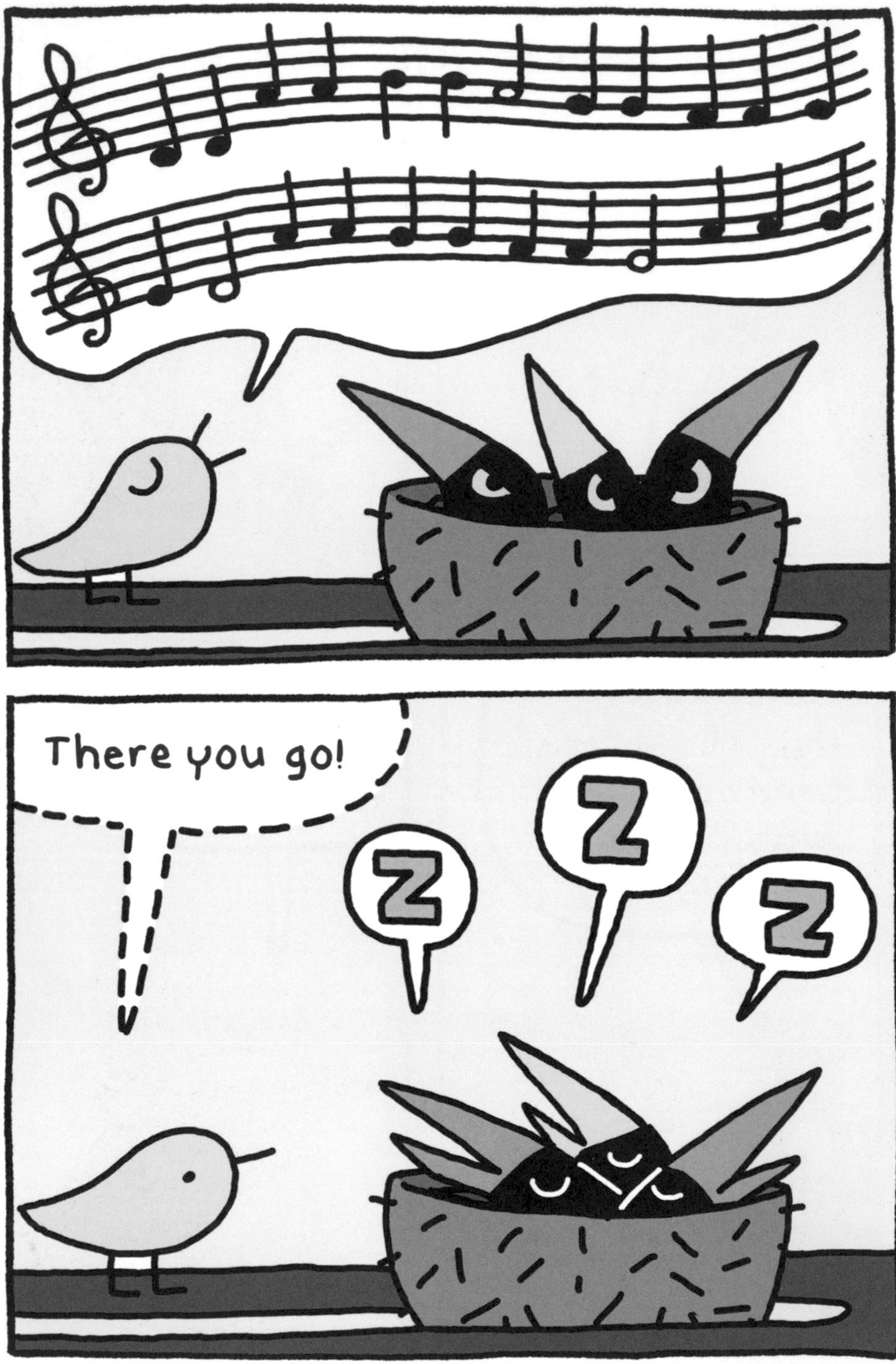
There you go!
Z
Z
Z

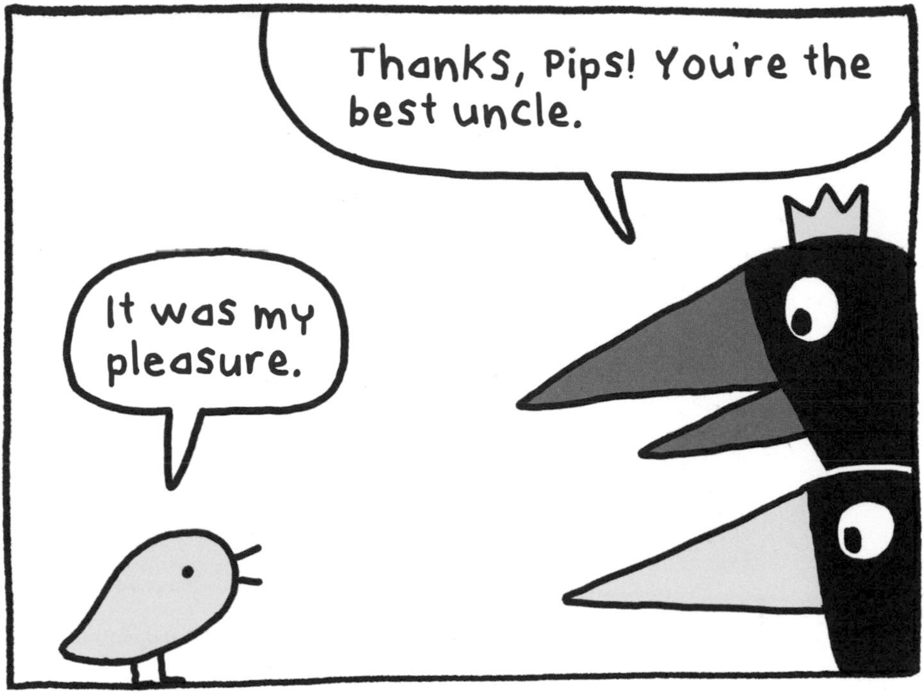
Thanks, Pips! You're the best uncle.
It was my pleasure.

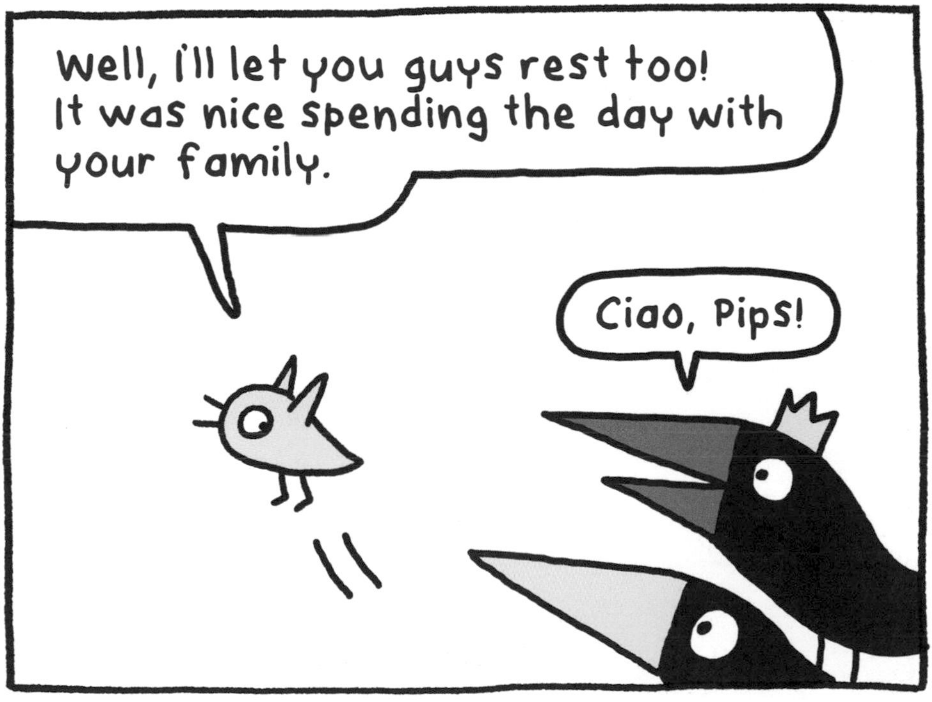
Well, I'll let you guys rest too! It was nice spending the day with your family.
Ciao, Pips!

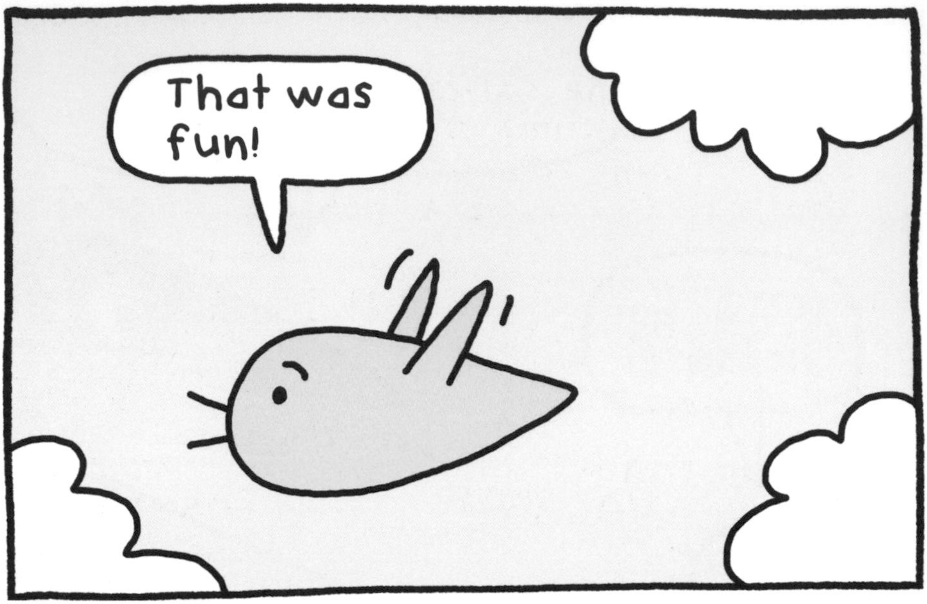
That was fun!

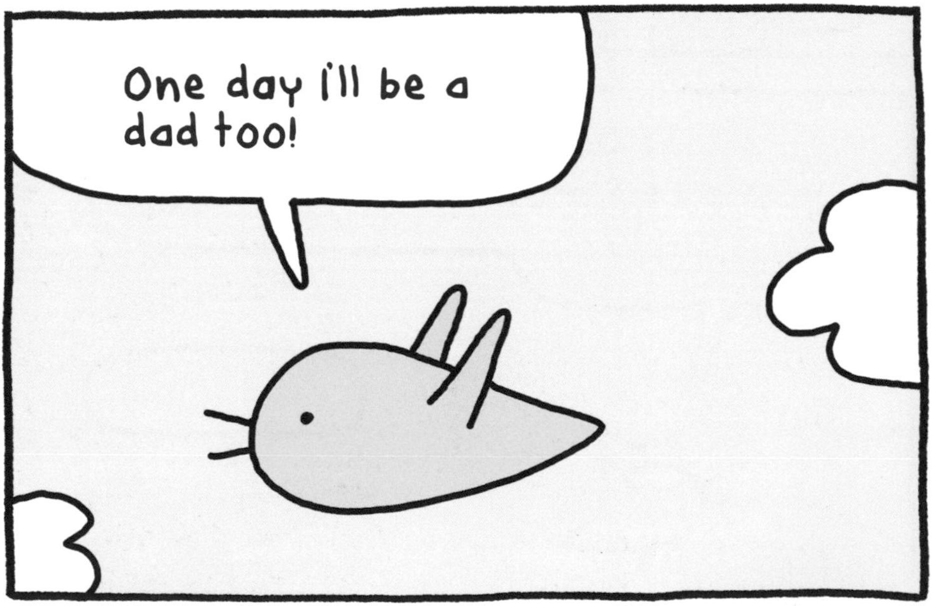
One day I'll be a dad too!

THE END

Note from the author:
While researching crows for this book, I found tons of cool facts that I didn't use. Here they are:

MORE CROW FACTS

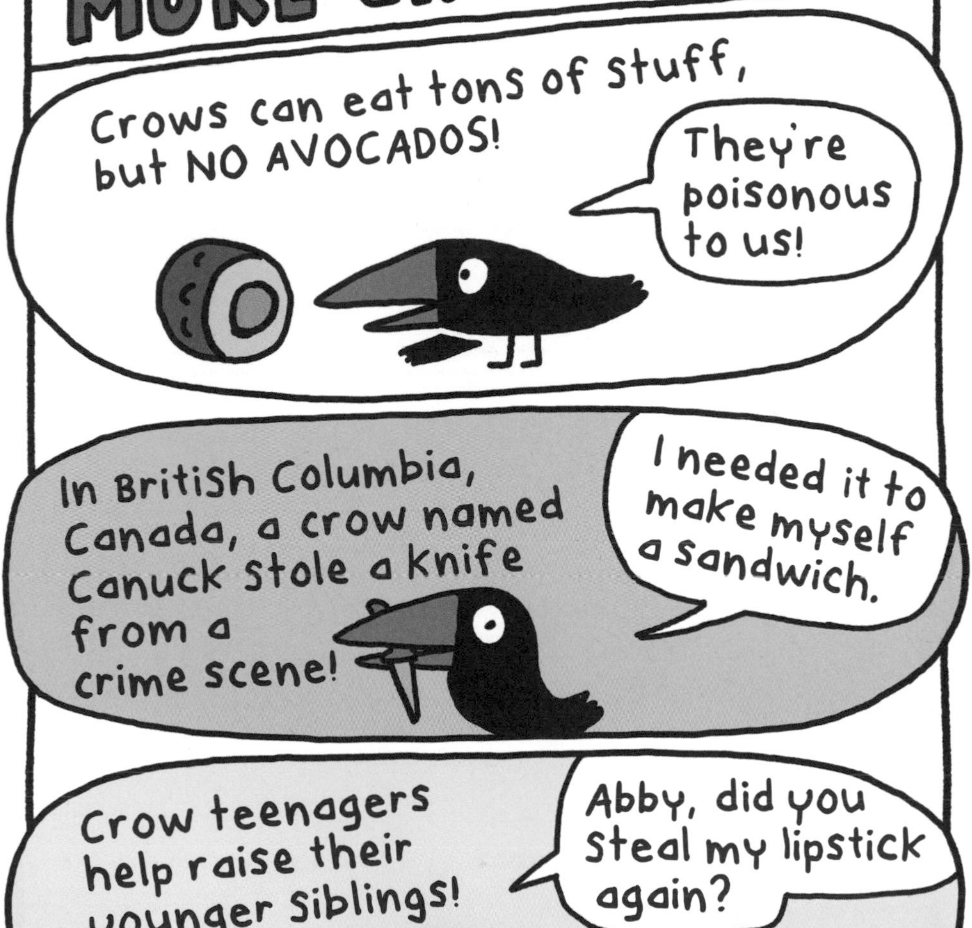
Crows can eat tons of stuff, but NO AVOCADOS!
They're poisonous to us!
In British Columbia, Canada, a crow named Canuck stole a knife from a crime scene!
I needed it to make myself a sandwich.
Crow teenagers help raise their younger siblings!
Abby, did you steal my lipstick again?

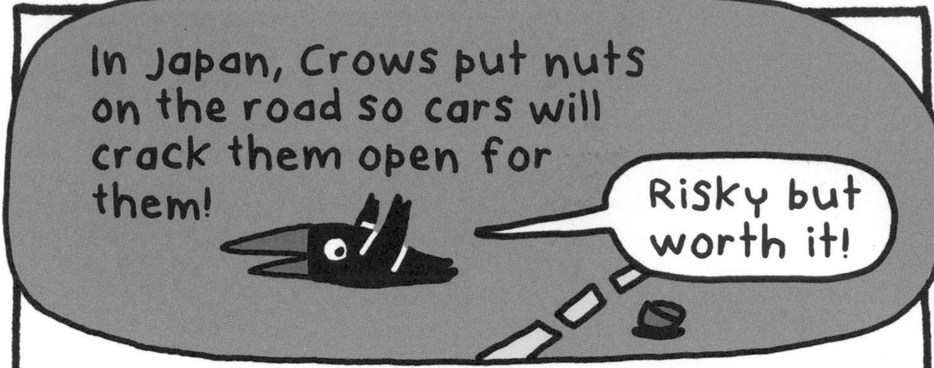
In Japan, crows put nuts on the road so cars will crack them open for them!
Risky but worth it!

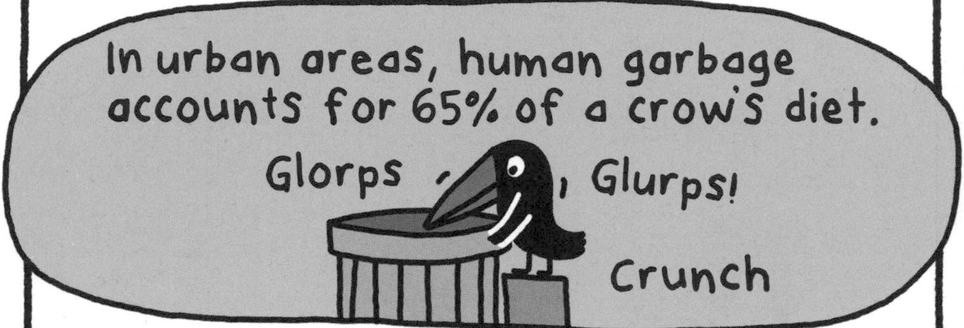
In urban areas, human garbage accounts for 65% of a crow's diet.
Glorps
Glurps!
Crunch

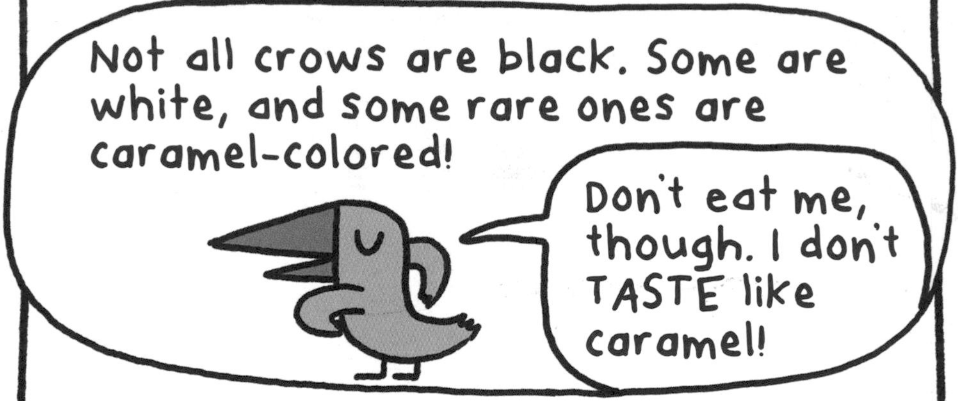
Not all crows are black. Some are white, and some rare ones are caramel-colored!
Don't eat me, though. I don't TASTE like caramel!

I hope that by now you like crows as much as I do! If you see one, say hi for me!

Elise Gravel